THE LEARNING CURVE

Recent Titles by Frances Paige from Severn House

THE LEARNING CURVE

Frances Paige

severn
House

This first world edition published in Great Britain 2007 by
SEVERN HOUSE PUBLISHERS LTD of
9–15 High Street, Sutton, Surrey SM1 1DF.
This first world edition published in the USA 2007 by
SEVERN HOUSE PUBLISHERS INC of
595 Madison Avenue, New York, N.Y. 10022.

British Library Cataloguing in Publication Data

Paige, Frances
   The learning curve
   1. Women novelists - Great Britain - Fiction
   2. Self-actualization (Psychology) in middle age - Fiction
   3. Country life - Great Britain - Fiction
   4. Life change events - Fiction
   I. Title
823.9'14 [F]

ISBN-13: 978-0-7278-6491-8

All Severn House titles are printed on acid-free paper.

Typeset by Palimpsest Book Production Ltd.,
Grangemouth, Stirlingshire, Scotland.
Printed and bound in Great Britain by
MPG Books Ltd., Bodmin, Cornwall.

One

'Do come in,' Kate said to the vicar's wife. The words rang like a bell in her head as she led the woman into her sitting room. It was Jan who'd used them when they had been discussing their plans after they had both accepted a voluntary redundancy payment from the publishing firm where they had been employed. Although the offer had been generous, privately they had blamed the accountants who had been brought in to boost the failing profits, but as they had both attained the ripe old age of fifty, they'd thought it wise to take the offer while it was open. The truth was that they had both become tired of the daily grind and unreliable Tube trains in winter, combined with the feeling that they were being outstripped by younger and more glamorous colleagues.

In Kate's case it was more involved. She and her boss, John Newton, had had an affair lasting for ten years. He was an attractive man, and she had genuinely fallen in love with him, despite being simply flattered at first by his advances. He had represented her adjustment to London, proof that she had shaken off and escaped from her early life in Scotland.

In the last few years, however, the affair had grown in her case, and possibly in his, rather tepid. He relished the fact that he had an 'out' at Kate's flat, being loath to leave his wife and children – more particularly the children, as Kate had discovered long ago, when she had begun to grow tired of his anecdotes of Annabel, his precocious

1

five-year-old daughter. She had never felt guilty about their relationship since Shirley, his wife, had a reputation for playing around. 'Give him up,' Jan had often advised.

But she felt she owed him something. He, it was, who on giving her a further trashy manuscript to read and edit, had said, 'More from Lily Rose. What is it you call her? Oh, yes, the Chanticleer. Why, I've never known.'

The reason was simple. Lily Rose, when she called in to talk over her current book, always reminded Kate of a cock – or a female cock, if there could have been any such thing. She had a huge bust straining the jacket buttoned tightly underneath it, and as if to balance, a huge rear, encased in a tight skirt, short enough to show her slim legs, tapering into splayed feet encased in high-heeled shoes. Her head seemed to nod incessantly as she emphasized her remarks.

After one of these occasions John had said to Kate, 'I'm sure you could write that stuff easily. Why don't you try?' She had. She had submitted a romance called *Love in Arcady*, and to her surprise, and more to John's, he said it was as good, or as bad, as Lily Rose's.

The result was that at the next meeting it had been passed for acceptance, and in due course, Kate had received a tidy sum, which she had promptly banked for her dream cottage in the country.

'It's an insult to you,' John had said, slightly miffed. 'You haven't searched your soul, just skated on the surface. You're capable of much better. I know you.' That was when Kate had realized that she had allowed herself to get into a situation that had been a mistake in every way; that her relationship with John had been for personal aggrandizement and not for genuine love. Yet still she couldn't bring herself to leave him – not yet.

Jan Cox was a widow and had a house in Streatham where she would remain after retirement, but Kate, still unmarried, had decided to give in to her secret longing for green fields, in comparison with her flat in Islington overlooking a grubby canal, and buy a country cottage with her nest egg. And give up John Newton. And write that novel, which would come from the depths of her soul.

She already knew what the subject would be. All she needed was time.

'I can just see you at your cottage door,' Jan had laughed. '"Do come in," you're saying to the vicar's wife. But at least I'm glad you've got rid of that bloodsucker!' Jan thought every man who came near you should propose marriage.

But no one had come along like Gavin . . .

'What a lovely room!' the woman said, looking around. 'These are the original houses of the village. Oak beams, and those French windows have been added. Such a sweet little garden! Ours is always cluttered with junk. We're an untidy family. I've always thought these cottages on the Green were my idea of bliss, not a rambling vicarage. And your wicket fence! Just right! The previous owner, Miss Thom, always seemed to be leaning over it. I can see her now, her stick and her white hair!'

'She's gone to a home in Worthing,' Kate said, stopping the woman mid-flow. Besides, she didn't like the analogy.

'I know, she was a dear old soul. It was your neighbour, Mrs Paxton, who told Ralph you had moved in, and he asked me to call. I'm Barbara, by the way, Barbara Dexter.' Your turn, her smile said.

'I'm Kate Armitage. Yes, I was lucky to find this cottage. I saw it on the Web, drove down and offered a price that was accepted, and here I am. I can hardly believe it. I worked in publishing for thirty years but decided to retire to the country.'

'If you can call this country. It's become commuter land, I'm afraid.'

'Still, the Green's nice, and there are fields with cows,

and a garden; everything I had dreamed of. Even an apple tree.'

'I expect you're like me. A country background. I worked in London till I got married, but my home was the West Country. You miss it.'

'Yes, I come from Scotland. My parents have died, and most of my friends have left, so there didn't seem much point in going back. Besides, I liked the thought of being near London, for the galleries.' It sounded in her ears like a prepared speech.

'Yes, that's the advantage here. An hour on the train. I go up quite often. Recently, since the boys are away and there's just Belle at home – she's fifteen – I've decided to return to teaching if I can get a post. Art is my subject. Do you know the Trossachs, then? Ralph and I spent our honeymoon at Loch Lomond, walking.'

'Yes, it's lovely. So near Glasgow, my hometown.'

'You won't find many hills round here; the Thames Valley is as flat as a pancake.'

'That should suit my advancing years quite well.' They both laughed.

'Isn't it terrible how one finds oneself in what I call the third part of one's life so soon? London does that to you, I think. Such a mad rush. My childhood was spent in the country, my girlhood was London, and now I'm into the third phase – the sliding downhill phase I call it, into the sere and yellow.'

Barbara Dexter looked at her. 'I'm presuming you're about the same age as I am, since you did a thirty-year stint in London?'

'All passion spent!' Kate was sorry she had said that. 'I'm fifty.'

'Me too. So now we know all about each other. There are only the blanks to fill in, if we want to.'

'I think we third-agers like to keep a bit to ourselves.'

'That's sixty-five, isn't it, *le troisième age*?'

'True.' They exchanged an amused look.

'Would you like some tea?' Kate asked her.

'I'd love some. Shall I come into the kitchen and help you?'

'No, thanks. Stay where you are.'

'That suits me beautifully. I'm naturally lazy.'

I think I'm going to like her, Kate thought as she prepared tea and found some biscuits, but I'll have to be careful and not confide too much.

When she returned to the sitting room, Barbara Dexer greeted her with her bright smile.

'I've just been composing a still life with that white vase on your table and the bowl of fruit. Van Gogh.'

'I picked the vase up at Portobello Market. I thought it looked Chinese.'

'It does. How nice this is!' She accepted a cup of tea, 'Yes, please. Milk but no sugar. To justify my barging in, Ralph said to tell you he'd be pleased to welcome you at church.'

Kate had already made up her mind on this one. 'I'm sorry. We weren't churchgoers as a family, my mother thought the people who went to the church nearest us formed a clique, or a talking shop – I'm sorry – ' she looked apologetically at Barbara Dexter – 'and I never got round to going to one in London, except a Christmas visit to St Paul's for the atmosphere and the singing. So it would be hypocritical to start now.'

'Fair enough. Unlike you, I was immersed from an early age. My father was a vicar, and Ralph was his curate before he got this parish. I never questioned the saintly life, but perhaps now that I'm into this third phase, and not having to set an example to the children, I'll give it room for thought. It's a good way of getting to know people, church, but I expect you won't find that difficult.'

'It's never been a problem, I'm not worried about that, although I'm unmarried and don't have children, which I realize would be an entrée here.'

5

'I don't think you'll need entrées. We're too near London here to try and compete with it. We used to have lots of societies – historical, etc. – but the only one that seemed to survive is the WI. I think the young, smart couples who come to live here like the touch of rusticity it gives. Then we have a crèche, which has a great appeal. Do I sound cynical?'

'Not at all, though I think it's always been like that – I mean with the young marrieds.' Though how should I know? she thought.

They talked easily for some time until Barbara Dexter suddenly looked at her watch. 'Goodness!' she said. 'Five fifteen! How time has flown!' She stood up. 'I promised Ralph I'd be back by five. He gets tired keeping an eye on Belle.' She smiled at Kate. 'I think you and I could go on for hours!'

'I've enjoyed meeting you,' Kate said, as she showed her out. 'Look in any time.'

The typical vicar's wife, she thought as she was in her kitchen rinsing the cups. Bright, but with a face she kept for her husband's parishioners. A lively talker and very much au fait with what went on in the village, and yet behind that was a shrewd intelligence. 'When the children were young I used to lock myself up in Ralph's study with *The Economist* and bar them entry. I simply had to get time for myself.' She had left, saying Kate was to look in at the vicarage any time. She would be more than welcome. If she wasn't there, Belle would tell Kate when she would be back.

Belle, Kate thought. Why was a young girl of fifteen hanging about the house? Shouldn't she be at school? Then she chastised herself: she had promised herself she wouldn't be drawn into idle village gossip or speculation.

She started to prepare her meal. She had determined that she would not make do as she often had in London with packaged meals, and that she would refer to the recipes she had written in a notebook ready for when she retired. She began cutting up vegetables for supper.

When she had finished she saw the sun was still shining in her garden. She poured herself a gin and tonic, put her prepared dish in the oven and went through the French windows carrying her drink. She settled herself in the wooden seat under the apple tree, surveying her territory from there, thinking, Yes, it was a good move, I'm going to like it here. She just hoped John wouldn't ferret her out.

Was Jan right, when she said Kate had wasted the best years of her life with him? She didn't think so. There had been some good times, and nothing was ever really wasted. She recognized that she had got into the relationship with John as a result of missing Gavin, and perhaps subconsciously to further her career. She let her mind drift back to Glasgow and her girlhood.

Her father had died when she was four years of age, and Margaret and Roy, her older brother and sister, had left home. She only realized why when she had grown up and was subject to the full battery of her mother's aggressive manipulation that had driven them away.

She and Gavin Armstrong had worked on a local newspaper, he a photographer and she a junior reporter. They were often sent on the same assignments, generally weddings. Perhaps propinquity had been the reason for falling in love. Gavin's ambitions were simple. He loved Kate. They should move in together, work hard, save up, then when they had enough money, take out a mortgage on a small house and start a family. The discussion was often set off at weddings that she had been detailed to write up and he to photograph.

The concept made her feel uncomfortable, although she loved him with all the passion of first love, but what about her wonderful career? She had always vowed to herself that she would leave home and work in London. It would be her escape route from her mother, who had become embittered at the loss of her husband and foisted her grudge against circumstances beyond her control on to her children; who in fact was paranoid, something that Kate didn't realize until much later.

She had begun applying for jobs in London before she met Gavin and worked with him on the newspaper. She had only been testing out the water, she told herself. When a large publishing firm offered her a job as an editorial assistant, she knew she had to come clean and tell her mother and Gavin.

It had been difficult. Telling Gavin had been bad enough. 'But I thought you loved me,' he had wailed.

'But I do! You know what she's like. I've got to get away!' Margaret and Roy felt the same. She stifles me, criticizes everything I do – you included. And if we get married she would be near us, I should have to visit her, and she would visit us, and I would never be free of her influence! You could leave with me, Gavin. You could find a job in London too. Yes, I know your parents are different. They would love our children. They wouldn't get in the way . . .'

The rows. The sitting in his car going over it and over it, the silences, the tears. 'It just means you don't love me enough.'

'I suppose it does, but I've got to get away.'

And then there was her mother's reaction. 'Mother, I've got a job in London—'

'What did you say?'

'I've got this wonderful job in London and—'

'Margaret has put you up to this. Or Roy. What have I done to deserve this? Left with three children to bring up and no help from anybody!'

'You're not the only woman left with children to bring up.' The fear rushing through her at her temerity, along with the niggling sympathy that was always there. Yes, it must have been hard, her young husband dying, but she had gone too far this time.

'You'd better watch your tongue, young lady, or you'll find yourself out on your ear, far less London.'

'Well, I'm going, whatever you say . . .'

Lying on her bed, sobbing, Kate knew that in the end she would have to get up, go into the kitchen and apologize to her mother's back.

Gavin came to see her regularly for the first year, but as her love for him dwindled because of the attractions of living in London on her own, she had told him that their affair was over.

'You were the only one for me,' he had said. It had been difficult forgetting his young, troubled face when he had said this and refraining from feeling that she had thrown away something valuable, which she would regret for ever. First love had been painful, but she knew her escape to London had been in fact an escape from her mother. And Gavin had been the loser.

Don't start regretting Gavin now, she told herself, looking around her new territory. You're going to fulfil yourself by writing.

Two

The bench under the apple tree was uncomfortable, and the table rickety. She'd have to replace them, and perhaps a little oasis could be made here, a 'feature' as it was called now, paved, beds of flowers and a pool with a fountain. And she could have more paving outside the French windows for outside dining.

What she needed was a garden designer with whom she could discuss plans, and perhaps Jan would come at the weekend and give her some advice – provided Nick, her partner, didn't mind. Privately Kate thought Nick was a mistake, but then she had to remember that Joe, Jan's husband, had died suddenly and left her with two children, and feeling lonely. When Kate had first met Nick, she had thought, No, no, he's a philanderer, looking for a soft billet . . . well, time would tell. It had, and after five years he was still there.

The gardens of the houses on each side of her were fortunately well-screened by lattice fencing and trees. Mrs Paxton on one side was probably indoors or in bed, but from the other side Kate could hear children playing. She hoped they were of school age and then she wouldn't have much disturbance . . . Don't become crabby, she told herself, you knew you would have neighbours. It won't be like the flat in Islington where you deliberately never got to know the other people around you.

But it had been easy to do there. Jan had warned her. 'Now that you're on your own, you have to have a definite policy or you'll find yourself being matey with all the wrong people, then you can't shake them off.' Jan spoke from the safety of her set-up in Streatham. Now Ros and Eve were married, and off her hands. And she was living with that sponger, Nick. Don't be unkind, Kate told herself. You know you haven't a big heart like Jan, and that you like your own company too much.

Sitting in the shade of the apple tree she suddenly felt a wave of loneliness sweep over her. The children had gone indoors, and there seemed to be a deathly hush now, so different from the steady background noise of London. The stillness of the countryside was surprising. She hadn't reckoned on this feeling. In London she always seemed to be rushing into the flat, or rushing out again for some appointment, with the background of traffic in her ears.

But you'll find things to do here, she assured herself. Drive to Leeston for the cinema, then there would be shopping during the day, perhaps some societies. Oh, she would keep herself busy, no doubt of that at all. And, of course, there was her writing, which would take first priority. She lifted her glass and drank the last of her gin and tonic, then walked down the flagged path towards the French windows of the lounge. Yes, table and chairs out here on a patio would do the trick.

She went in and went through the lounge into the kitchen. When she turned on the lights it sparkled at her, the white surfaces gleaming. There was a tempting smell coming from the oven. She'd eat here tonight, but she wouldn't make a habit of it. No slopping about, she had told herself. A properly set table. With this in mind she took out a bottle of Sauvignon Blanc from the refrigerator and placed it on the table, found a glass. She turned on the radio. Eating in the Islington flat had never seemed as lonely as this. But, then, there had been John.

She poured herself a glass of wine and took the dish out of the oven and placed it on the table. She took a plate from the rack and sat down. This was it. Her first night in her own house. She took the lid off the dish – a kind of oven risotto. She'd never eat all this on her own tonight.

After her meal Kate locked up and went upstairs. She went into the small room at the back of the house which she had set up as her office, turned on the computer to see if there were any emails for her, then sat looking at the screen. She typed in '*My Father, Robert Armitage, born 1914.*'

She sat for a long time, making random jottings. She had been between four and five when her father had died, and she could only surmise his life before that. She knew that he had been one of two brothers – there had been a sister also, called Isobel. When the father, her grandfather, had died, he had left the farm to George, the elder brother, and Robert, her father, had been in India and Burma during the War.

All she was aware of was that there had been no communication with her uncle at the farm, which her mother described as 'a big place, Manor Farm, part of the Belmorris Estate'. Kate had grown up aware that the early part of her mother and father's life was buried in the past, not to be talked about.

Margaret had married young and had left home after a hasty marriage, and Roy, Kate's brother, had done the same. He was now living in Leeds with his wife, Karin, and their family. Kate remembered being dressed up as a bridesmaid to Margaret, and only came to realize when she was in her teens, and had made friends at school, how dominated by her mother she had been and what a soulless life they had led compared with others. Although Margaret and Roy had escaped from their mother's dominance into marriage, she had realized that, despite her love for Gavin, that route was not for her.

So here I am, she thought, fifty years of age, not sure that I took the right course, but at least I have a goal now: to explore my father's life, and possibly find a meaning for my own.

Had the success with the romantic novel been a fluke? she wondered. And had she the capacity to write a 'real' novel? Far away she heard the hoot of an owl, or at least that's what she thought it was. Writing was so ephemeral. What one typed didn't always portray one's thoughts; one had to try and try, till it looked and felt right. Why had the romantic novel flowed so easily from her fingers? Because she hadn't had to try? Had John really meant it, when he had said that she was capable of more? In the still of the night – twelve thirty – she checked her watch. No time really in London . . . taxis and cars would be darting about, buses lumbering through Islington, restaurants buzzing. What was she doing in this outlandish place where there was only the sound of a solitary bird?

What she had to do fairly soon, Kate thought, was to get in touch with Margaret, and see if she could tell her if there was anyone in their parents' village who could fill in the early gaps of their father's life. Margaret would be amused if she knew that her 'wee sister' was embarking on such a project. Margaret had always treated her as the baby sister, and been slightly surprised at her move to London, although she understood the reason. She had thought Gavin had been just right for her.

Stop procrastinating, she told herself. If you're going to do it, start now . . .

So after clearing up in the kitchen Kate telephoned her sister. She should have done it long ago, she realized, as she waited for her call to be answered. She heard the Scottish tones of her sister's voice.

'Hello, who is it?'

'Margaret, it's Kate. How are you?'

'We're really well here. Although we've had a lot of rain. Well, you know Glasgow. What have you been up to? It's ages since we heard from you.'

'Remember I told you I was looking for a house out of London?'

'Yes. Have you had any luck? The houses here are much cheaper than the south. We have a friend who is an estate agent, and they're building really nice flats on the docks, just like London.'

'I didn't want a flat. I wanted a garden. Well, I've found a cottage off the beaten track, in a small village a little over an hour from London, a snip, really, because the old lady who owned it needed a quick sale to pay for her nursing home bills, the solicitor said, and I got ahead of the queue and had the money handy. I'll give you my telephone number and address when we've finished speaking, and I'll send you a card when I get round to it.'

'You're the limit, Kate. I never know what you'll get up to next.'

'Well, as you know, I was never allowed to think for myself when mother was alive, so I've got to do it now.'

'Don't I know it? Roy is doing well in Leeds now. James and I visited them recently. You should see their house! Karin has gone to town on it. She's been good for Roy. She gives me a ring occasionally. As a family we've never been good communicators.'

'That's true. I've got another reason for phoning you, Margaret. Remember I sent you a copy of a romantic novel I wrote?'

'Gosh, yes. That was hot stuff. I read out the spicy bits to James. He was shocked. But then men always are. They don't like it spelled out.'

'Well, a friend of mine advised me to write another book, one that might appeal to your James, had this friend known him. "From the soul," he said. Believe it or not, I was paid well for the romantic novel, which provided the money to buy this little house at an outrageous price, and I've started another book. It's to be devoted to our father, whom I barely remember, just a presence in my early life, but you'll have more memories. You'd have been about ten when he died. Could I ask you to search your mind for any recollections of him?'

'Hey, hold on, wee sister! I'm not a writer!'

'No, but you always had a good memory. Would you try, Margaret, please? If you like I'd come to Glasgow and bring my laptop.'

'Well, I could try.'

'I'd dedicate the book to you. You'd see your name in print.'

'That's not a treat. I see my name printed often. You know I'm on numerous committees here.'

'Yes, I'd forgotten how important you are. Another thing, Margaret, is there anyone in the village where our grandparents lived who would be able to give me some background information about the family? It's our father and his brother I'm particularly interested in.'

'Well, there's a sister, Isobel, but I don't know where she lives now. Possibly in a home. Or she may have died. She always was a bit . . . peculiar, never having been married.'

'I'd better look out.'

'You were supposed to resemble Isobel. That copper hair, and the blue eyes.'

'I believe she was quite a beauty.'

'No fishing. I've thought of someone. There's Cathy Livingstone in the library. She knew everything and everybody there.'

'Have you got her address?'

'And her telephone number, if you want it.'

'That would be great! Would she mind if I phoned?'

'Not Cathy. There's nothing Cathy likes more than a good blether.'

'You've helped me a lot, Margaret. I will try and visit you. It's not that I don't think of you and Roy often – and James, of course.'

'Away with you! But I know what you're like and take

you as I find you. Goodness knows what you got up to in London, but to write books! I think that's really great. And I'll search my mind for you and put it down. I've got a computer now, so I can send you an email. I know you won't come to Glasgow.'

'I would Margaret, honest.' I sound like the wee sister now, she thought.

She hung up and immediately dialled the number Margaret had given her. She heard a piercing female voice. 'Hello, who is it?'

'It's Kate Armitage. Margaret tells me you're still in touch with her.'

'Yes, we are. I'm still in the library, although I'm due to retire this month. Her wee sister, is it? Who went to London?'

'That's me.'

'Yes, I remember you, Kate. You were a great reader, Margaret told me.'

'Yes, under the bedclothes! Well, this may surprise you, Cathy, I'm writing a book about my father, and I wanted some information about his background. I never visited my uncle with my mother when I was at home. And then, as you say, I went to London. Could you tell me about the farm where my father was brought up? I was three or four when he died, so never really knew him.'

'No, you're right. Your mother never visited here after that. She had a grudge against everything and everybody. Your grandfather, your father's father, lived in what was called the Manor Farm with his wife and family. He was quite a gentleman. People called him the Colonel. They had two sons, George and Robert. And a daughter, Isobel. She never married. George inherited the farm, and Robert was in the war in Burma for two or three years. That was your father. Then he came back to Manor Farm. It was rumoured Anne Kay, your mother, had haunted the farm at one time, putting Isobel's back up. And Isobel blamed her for the trouble between Robert and George. She was never away from the farm, chasing George. She had hoped to run the house for him.'

'Anne and George? Surely you mean Robert, my father's name was Robert—'

'Aye, but before she married Robert, Anne was chasing his brother – your uncle George.'

Kate was stunned. Suddenly things began to make sense – like why her family had never visited Manor Farm when she was growing up. She tried to steer the conversation, her heart thumping.

'So you think Isobel was jealous of Anne?'

'Aye, that's right. They were good friends, the girls, but I don't know if Isobel ever knew that Anne's mother was in a lunatic asylum. The next thing was that Anne and Robert were getting married.'

This news about her mother's mother – her grandmother – surprised Kate. She had always supposed she had an incurable disease. Inheritable? Did that explain her mother's behaviour from which they'd all suffered? Margaret and Roy had never known, and their grandfather had died without the family ever knowing him. Her father wasn't here to ask.

Cathy continued, 'I knew your mother was difficult to deal with, and the next time Margaret and I got together was after she married James Stewart, a nice man, but your mother didn't approve of him. She told me once that your mother seemed to change after your father died, and she was glad to get away from her. George never married. Maybe Anne thought he would propose when his brother died.

'Then Roy got married to Karin somebody-or-other, who persuaded him to go to Leeds, where she lived . . . they had met at university. Margaret's the one to tell you about their life at home before she married. I gathered it wasn't a bed of roses. But you were the little sister. You probably didn't understand.'

All I understood, Kate thought, was that we, as a family, were victims of Mother's peculiar attitude to us all. 'No, Cathy, I didn't understand, but I think I do now.'

'And you're thinking of writing a book about your father? Well, you wouldn't remember much about him since you were so young when he died. I always liked your father. Good-looking and great fun, unlike George who was quiet and deep. But not the marrying kind – as no doubt your mother found out.'

'You've told me quite a lot, Cathy, and I'm very grateful to you. If I need any more information, may I phone you again?'

'I'll write to you first and give you my home address. I'm thinking of moving back to Glasgow. Before I leave the library I can use the equipment there, if you send me your email address.'

'That's good of you. Thank you very much.'

'No bother, as they say. It's quite nice to be associated with an author. Although I've been surrounded with books, I've never thought to write one. I guess authors are born, not made.'

Kate hung up, her ears ringing. So her mother had been in love with George before she married Robert. And Anne's mother – Kate's grandmother – had been in some kind of home for the mentally unstable. If it were a hereditary condition, it would explain a lot . . .

Kate got into bed with a lot to think about, knowing she'd take a long time getting to sleep.

Isobel woke with the pleasant feeling that today was very special. From her bedroom she could hear the voices of George and Old Bob, who came in very early in the morning to see to the milking, the sluicing out of the byre and the tidying up of the yard behind the house. She could hear the sound of the yard brush being used by Old Bob's son, Bobby, who helped his father and was being taught the duties that would be required of him when his father retired. 'He'll do his best, sir,' old Bob had promised George.

She got quickly out of bed, put on her dressing gown and went to peep out of her window. Yes, there was George, in his yard clothes, clean shirt and old leather jacket, and that squashed felt hat that he refused to jettison. You'd think he'd dress better, she thought, when his brother is coming home from the War today. George looked up, saw her, and took off his hat to wave it at her in a triumphant gesture. Yes, he was just as excited as her. She saw him go into the coach house, heard the old Buick start up, and quickly left the window and made her way to the bathroom to wash and dress. She was in the kitchen helping Mary, Bob's wife, to prepare breakfast when George came in.

'Aye, you'll be all excited this morning, Mr George,' Mary said from the old stove, which she wouldn't allow George to throw away. 'I'm just seeing to your porridge.'

19

'*Yes, it's a great day, Mary,*' *George said.* '*Rob was always a favourite of yours.*'

'*Now you know me, Mr George. Ah never made favourites o' any o' you, but these golden curls! They'll hae broken many o' yon black wumman's hearts where he's been fighting.*'

'*Sure enough, Mary, and he'll probably have a trail of wee black bairns after him.*' *He looked at Isobel, and she threw up her eyes to the ceiling, She was standing at the electric cooker (Mary's* bête noir*) preparing eggs and bacon for his breakfast.*

'*Don't put the fear of God in Mary,*' *she said. And to the woman,* '*They have olive skins in Burma, Mary, golden, not black.*' *She dished up the eggs and bacon on to a plate, and put it in front of her brother where he was sitting at the table.* '*Ten minutes, George, and we'll have to get going.*'

'*You may be right,*' *Mary said over her shoulder,* '*aboot they black wummen, but I'm sure they'll be fatter than you wi' nae breakfast inside ye.*'

'*Mind your own business, I'm having toast and coffee. I don't want to be sick in the car going to Glasgow. You know the rate George goes at.*'

In the car later beside George, Isobel's mind turned to Anne Kay. I bet she looks in to see Robert, she thought. She was never away from the farm these days, chasing George. She'd always been fond of Robert, but despite that, she had begun to frequent the farm, on the pretext of calling for Isobel.

Isobel hadn't forgotten that afternoon a month ago when she had returned from shopping. Mary wasn't in the kitchen. She could hear her in the outhouse pumping the water, which had to be done each day to supply the household needs. Her father had clung to the practice, refusing all offers to have water led into the house, and George had humoured him in the last days of his illness.

Sentimentally, he had left things as they were although it was a year since their father had died.

No one about, she had thought, seeing George's old hat lying on the chair where he usually dropped it when he came in from the farm. She heard someone coming downstairs and when she looked up, Anne Kay was in the doorway. Her dark eyes had a peculiar light in them, as if they were illuminated from behind.

'Oh, Isobel,' she said, 'I've been upstairs using your bathroom. I called round to see if you would make up a four at tennis with the Dalton sisters. There was no one about, so I took the liberty . . .' Isobel had noticed that as she spoke, she was smoothing her dress with both hands.

'That's all right, Anne,' she said, 'I got back early. But I've a lot to do. I haven't time to play tennis, even with the Dalton sisters. Sorry!' She began emptying shopping from her basket.

'OK, not to worry. They're not in your league, anyhow. I'll make myself scarce, then.' Again Isobel noticed her strange eyes. 'Well, I'll say chin-chin. Let me know if you want to see that film at Hamilton next week.' It had been about an hour before George appeared.

'When will supper be ready, Isobel?' he had asked. She searched his face. It was inscrutable.

'Half an hour. Did you know Anne Kay had been in the house?'

He raised his eyebrows. 'No? I was busy at my desk paying accounts. I had a spare hour.'

'She called to see me, and went upstairs to use our facilities.' She laughed, keeping her eyes on his. They were steady, meeting hers, but she noticed a muscle at the corner of his mouth twitching.

'A long way to come for that,' he said, giving a short laugh.

'She was here to ask me to make up a four for tennis. But I said I was too busy.'

'Right.' He lifted his hat from the chair and screwed it on his head, the way he did, pulling the brim forward over his eyes. 'Better be going to see to the milking. What time's supper?'

'I just told you, half an hour – around eight?'

'OK.' She watched him go out. Slim hips, she thought.

She wasn't sick, fortunately, despite George's fast driving, the triangular black shapes of the coal bings flashing by. Mining had desecrated the countryside around Glasgow. Steel had taken its place, with Colville's huge drums seen for miles around. Still, the Lanarkshire villages clung on, fighting against becoming suburbs of Glasgow.

Now they were over the Jamaica Bridge and turning off Gordon Street into the dark tunnel leading into Central Station. They parked the car. There seemed to be more bustle than usual around the London platform.

'There he is!' She clutched George's arm as they watched Robert, attended by a porter who was pushing a laden trolley.

'No black bairns,' George said, and then they were at the barrier, and helping Robert get his trolley through, patting him, the two men shaking hands, she landing kisses on Robert's cheek.

'Oh, Robert, safe and sound,' she said breathlessly. 'The car's parked near.' She was stealing glances as they walked, at this brother of hers, so handsome, so different, tanned, jaunty in his captain's uniform, with a different air about him which seemed to say, 'I have lived . . .'

The homecoming was a triumph, with all the employees lined up waiting to shake Robert's hand, and then the sumptuous supper that a speechless

Mary had cooked in readiness, and then a tour round the 'policies', as they were always called.

'Lord Balmorris still in residence?' Robert asked George.

'Yes, but not so good these days. Gout. But he wants you to go round and see him.'

Then a trip to the far field to see Robert's pride and joy, his Aberdeen Angus cattle, which had been faithfully tended while he was away.

They were on the towpath at the Morris river, Robert drinking in the familiar sights and sounds, when they heard the tinkle of a bicycle bell behind them. When Isobel turned she saw that it was Anne, and that she had dismounted and was wheeling her bicycle towards them. 'What a surprise!' she was saying. 'Back safe and sound, Robert. You look great! I know where to go now if I want a tan! I have to kiss the returning hero.' She flung her arms round him, standing on tiptoe to do so. Robert looked embarrassed, and when Isobel looked at George, she saw him turn his head away.

'Come back to the house with us, Anne,' Isobel said, wondering why she said it. 'We'll be having a cup of coffee. I'm afraid you've missed the champagne.'

She demurred, smiling. 'I have my bike . . .'

'I'll push it for you,' Robert said, and then he and Anne were walking in front of George and Isobel, who were listening to their chatter. At least George was silent, a stony silence. Damn Anne Kay, Isobel thought, I might have known she would push herself in somehow.

In the house they all laughed and talked a great deal. George had rustled up a bottle of whisky, which helped to dispel any uneasiness on Isobel's part. Anne obviously enjoyed the two men teasing her and encouraged it by her provocative manner, but when she said she must go, it was George who said he would see her home, that it was too late for her to be cycling alone through the village. Anne, although she put on an appearance of reluctance, gave in. Isobel remembered that she was given a very free rein by her father. There were only the two of them as her mother had been in a home for a long time. The whole thing was a mystery. No one knew what was wrong with her. Anne's father had met her mother in Glasgow, where they had married and lived. When his parents had died and left him the family house, he had come to live there with his daughter, Anne, but minus a wife who was permanently ill – with an incurable disease, was what was given out – and was in a home, and although there was gossip, the village soon accepted Mr Kay with his small daughter and housekeeper. The fact that he travelled to Glasgow by the business train to his architect's job in the city gave him credence.

When they had left, Robert asked Isobel, 'Is there something between those two?'

'Goodness knows,' she said. 'She plays her cards close to her chest, Anne Kay, although she's supposed to be my best friend, and you know George, you can't get anything out of him.'

But she was glad to have Robert to herself, and that she could ask him about his experiences in Burma. He told her about being trapped in the Admin Box just after he arrived, and showed her maps, and told her about his batman to whom he had been devoted, and about the bungalow and servants that had been allocated to him; in fact about the life of Reilly he had led. Not all of the time – he had been damned lucky to come through it all without a scratch. He had driven about in a jeep, but the life he painted for her was far removed from the slog and horror of what he must have gone through.

The Learning Curve

'The worst thing,' he said, 'is losing friends you have grown to love. And yes, we felt we were forgotten. We all perked up when we heard of Hitler's death. We knew it wouldn't be long before we were given the attention we deserved. And then there was Hiroshima . . . I suppose that was a good thing . . .'

Isobel was in bed when she heard the door slam, then for a long time there was the rumble of two male voices downstairs. It seemed a friendly rumble.

Three

The next day Kate was up bright and early, and after setting the cottage to rights and having lunch she decided to walk round the village to get her bearings. She felt she had made a good start with the book and that she should let it 'settle'. She could see Manor Farm and its environs in her mind, and the people there, like an alternative landscape to the one she inhabited. The Anne Kay she had imagined seemed a far cry from the mother she had known, who could be humorous at times, but it was often a cruel and disparaging humour. Why had she become like that?

Kate set off, clicking the wicket gate satisfactorily behind her. She passed the village hall, surrounded by fields in which a few cows were grazing. She saw a substantial farmhouse in the background, skirted by a few old houses, with impressive sounding names on the gates. On the other side of the road was the village Green. She could see to the far side of it, where there was the outline of more houses. The green was obviously a square. She would have to do some exploring. She continued walking and then came to what she thought might be called the heart of the village, a garage and a post-office-cum-village-store.

A man in front of the garage in overalls, who was working on a car, raised his hand to her and called, 'Nice morning.' There were a few women standing talking outside the post office and she felt their eyes on her as she went in. There were some people at the grocery side, where a grey-haired man officiated. She went to the post office counter as she wanted stamps. The woman there was pleasant. 'You're a new face here,' she smiled, and when Kate told her she had come to live in Miss Thom's house, she said, 'Ah, yes, poor Miss Thom. She went off her legs, and had to be removed to a nursing home by her niece. I'm afraid it's our turn next. We've begun to think of retiring. My husband over there is sixty now and I'm not far behind.'

'You don't look it,' was all Kate could think of by way of reply. She crossed to the other counter and made a few purchases. The husband was quite jocular, saying that he hadn't seen her before and they could do with some new blood in the village. She noticed that his eyes rolled appreciatively as she paid him.

When she went out of the shop she saw that she had reached a corner where a road ran off the main road of the village. Its name, fixed on a stone wall, was scarcely discernable. 'Lansdown Lane', she managed to read, and underneath there was a painted notice board that read 'M. Leaver, Plants'. She thought the stone wall might possibly be enclosing a large house, because of the branches of trees showing above it, and some tall chimneys.

She decided to investigate, and began walking down Lansdown Lane, which was in fact a rough, unmade road bordered by large, new-looking houses, intended, she thought, for the smart, young couples whom Barbara Dexter had talked about. No doubt when the road was levelled it would look quite desirable here, but more suburban. Still, that was what they wanted. How villages lose their character, she thought.

When she came to the place selling plants, she found it to be a large enclosure, bordered by fencing. Apart from a few beds of plants and various pieces of equipment lying about, she could see the enclosure was mostly composed of greenhouses, and in one of them a man was busy with a watering can. He looked up and saw Kate hesitating at the gate. Opening the door, he came towards her. 'Hello!' he said. 'Can I help you?'

She saw a middle-aged, good-looking man, with the red-brown hair that goes with a freckled skin. His eyes had a sad expression in comparison with his cheerful greeting.

'I hope so,' she said. 'I've come to live in the village. In Miss Thom's old house. Perhaps you know it?'

'Miss Thom . . .' he repeated. 'Facing the Green? I've supplied plants to her.'

'Good,' Kate said. 'I want to lay out part of the garden with flags, and make an area for sitting in. Can you help me?' She noticed that while he was listening, his face fell into a sad expression, matching that of his eyes, and there were downward lines running from his mouth, now that his smile had disappeared.

'I don't do any structural work myself,' he said, 'but I could plan it for you. I know a man who is good at flagging.'

'That would be ideal. Could we fix a time for you to call and see what I'm needing?' she asked.

'Certainly. I'm thinking of Garry Fox in Nettlebed Lane. I'll contact him today, and bring him to your house. Shall we say on Monday, about ten thirty?'

'I'll make that suit,' she said. 'Monday, ten thirty. Thanks.'

She was turning to go away, when he said, 'Did you notice the pub at the corner, the Hare and Hounds?'

'I think so.' She was puzzled.

'If you happen to be in it sometime – they do very good grub   have a look at their garden with tables at the back. I designed that with Garry.'

'I'll try to do that.' She smiled and left him, walking briskly. He was the type of man with whom casual conversation would be difficult, she thought, and she didn't feel like trying. Nevertheless, she noted the Hare and Hounds as she passed.

In the afternoon, she decided to do some further exploring. She would find Nettlebed Lane and have a look around. It must be on the other side of her cottage as she hadn't passed it on the way to the village shops. She would enjoy having another walk out, then in the evening there would be her meal to cook and a phone call to Jan. She had never had to plan her day like this before. It was strange.

Nettlebed Lane gave the impression of a country lane, probably a reflection of the village as it once had been. There were frequent open spaces, fields, farms and a row of council houses incongruously set in the middle of the lane, obviously tenanted, because there were children playing outside them and men working in their gardens. Some gave her a greeting, a gaggle of women who were chatting together looked curiously at her.

Gradually the houses petered out, as did the road, changing to a dirt path that ran through some scrubby land thick with nettles, which was fenced off. When they became difficult to pass through she decided to turn back. Ahead of her and coming towards her she saw the figure of a man who was swishing at the nettles with a stick. When he came near her she saw he was young with long hair and a thin, aquiline face with a prominent nose. He had to stand aside to let her pass, and feeling apprehensive she raised her eyes and said, 'Good afternoon.'

'Nice day,' he said. He was smiling, but the smile hadn't reached his eyes.

When she got back she had to think what to do next. Strange, she thought again, having so much time to spare. Perhaps that was what retirement meant.

She went into the kitchen and made a cup of tea, then took out a quiche from the freezer, and left it on the counter to defrost. Now a salad. She prepared it, covered it with

Frances Paige

cling film, then went to her sitting room where the telephone was. Jan was in and her cheerful voice was good to hear.

'How's the country girl doing?'

'Surviving. I've spoken to one man today about my garden, then had a walk in Nettlebed Lane – yes, that's what it's called – where I met another man. So different from Islington where you're falling over them.'

'Don't tell me you're actually missing the noise and bustle of London, and men?'

'Not at all, it's a pretty village and I've met the vicar's wife, as you predicted.'

'Good. You'll be in the social whirl in no time.'

'I'll be surprised if that exists. There's certainly no sign of it. Maybe when all the young at heart get home from London. Jan, could you come to stay this weekend?'

'Sorry, sweetie, Nick and I are going to friends on Sunday for dinner.'

'Well, how about you driving down on Saturday, and I'll take you to lunch in the local pub? Bring Nick, of course,' she added, hoping she didn't sound too reluctant.

'Why not? Oh, no, he goes to his swimming club on Saturday. But yes, I'll come without him on Saturday. I'd like to see your house, and have a good old natter.'

'Great! It's easy to find. It's just about a quarter of a mile past the shops, on the main road, facing the Green. "Rose Cottage" it's called.'

'How sweet. Is there a duck pond too?'

'Haven't seen it yet. We can explore together.'

'Right. I'll set off early and try to be with you at eleven.'

'Great. I'll have the coffee ready. Give my love to Nick. I'm sorry he can't come.'

'Sure. It'll do him good to be left.'

Kate's heart lifted when she saw Jan park her car at the wicket gate. Dear old Jan, always able to find her way

30

anywhere, competent, black-suited, bleached hair, neat legs, high heels. Nick wouldn't feel younger than her, she was ageless.

She flung open the door. 'Eleven on the dot.' They kissed.

'I took a wrong turning out of Berkhamsted, but got straight afterwards. This is nice, Kate. Your mother's furniture looks good here. And your father's clock on the mantelpiece. A nice little garden.' She had moved to the French windows.

'I've got plans for it. The pub we're going to for lunch is supposed to give me ideas. It was the garden designer man who told me to look at their back garden.'

'Good. Supposing you pour the coffee – I see you have it ready – while I go to the loo, then we can set off.'

After a quick coffee and a catch-up, they went in Kate's car, and parked in front of the pub. When they went in they found it busy with the tables well filled. A man detached himself from the crowd at the bar and came towards them. Handsome, Kate thought, but too sure of himself. She noticed his swagger. A drinker. Purple-red complexion. 'Good morning, ladies, can I help you?'

'We'd like a table for lunch, please,' she said.

'Certainly. There's a nice table for two vacant at the end. Follow me.'

They fell in behind his checked jacket. The split at the back showed his rear encased in brown corduroy trousers. 'Here we are.' He placed them at a small table looking on to a paved garden.

'Can I fetch you a drink, ladies?'

'Jan?' Kate said.

'I think I'd like a dry white wine. I must say it's nice to be waited on like this. It doesn't happen in London.'

'We're more polite in the country.' He smiled.

'You're not a gastropub, then,' Kate said.

'God forbid!' he said. 'We're old-fashioned here. And

what can I bring you?' he asked, turning his attention to Kate.

'I think we'll celebrate with a bottle. Sauvignon Blanc OK, Jan?'

She nodded. 'But only a sandwich for me, Kate.' She smiled at the man. 'We have to keep our figures.'

'And very nice too.' His look was appreciative. He indicated a menu lying on their table. 'Have a browse while I get your bottle. There's a good selection there.'

They looked at each other when he had gone.

'The owner?' Jan said, eyebrows lifted.

'I think so.'

'And the woman behind the bar, his wife?'

'Possibly.'

'The original blowsy blonde?'

Unfair, Kate thought. Although the woman was blonde, it might well be her natural colour. Her complexion was pink and white. She looked pleasant, and was laughing and chatting with the customers. When the man came back with the bottle and was pouring their drinks, he smiled at both of them. 'I haven't had the pleasure of seeing you here before. You're strangers in the district?'

'I've come to live here,' Kate said. 'My friend is visiting me.'

'You couldn't have come to a nicer village.' He looked at Kate. 'Can I take your order?'

They had discussed what they would eat.

'Soup of the day and a sandwich each, please.'

'Good choice. I can recommend the soup today – carrot and coriander.'

When they had chosen their sandwich and he had gone away, they turned their attention to the view from the window.

'That's the garden the man told me to have a look at. It was designed by him.'

'Nice,' Jan said. 'I like the flagging. Much nicer than those horrid red bricks.'

When they were comfortably chatting and sipping their wine, Kate happened to raise her head and recognized the man coming towards their table. It was the owner of the gardens in Lansdown Lane. Their glances met and he stopped, smiling.

'I've come to say hello,' he said. 'I saw you from the bar.'

'Did you? My friend and I have come to see your handiwork.'

'I'm glad Cyril placed you where you could see it. He's the landlord here – at least his wife is. Cyril and Judy Grantham.'

'We'll have a look at it on our way out,' Kate said.

There was an awkward pause. She couldn't remember his name.

'Well, I'll call on Monday, as arranged,' he said, looking uncomfortable.

'Yes, of course.' She felt Jan looking at her. He seemed to hesitate for a moment, then bowed and walked away.

'I think he wanted to be introduced,' Jan said.

'I think so. To tell you the truth, I couldn't remember his name.'

'Not to worry.'

Kate drove round the Green back to her cottage, so that they could see the extent of the village. At the far side of the Green there was a cricket match in progress. When they were on the opposite side to the pub Kate saw a sign, 'The Vicarage', on the gate of an old stone house. Before she turned into the main road where her cottage was, they passed a perfectly respectable duck pond, with one duck paddling apparently happily in it.

'There be your duck pond,' Jan said, and as they reached Kate's cottage, 'I think it's all very nice, Kate. I'm sure you'll be happy here. Quite a few houses too, clustered round the Green. Once you get to know some people, who's to say?'

Dear old Jan, Kate thought, desperate to get me hitched.

Four

The next morning Kate was up bright and early to be ready for Mr Leaver. She had remembered his name. He arrived punctually with the man whom he had spoken about. She recognized the stranger immediately as the one she had passed in Nettlebed Lane. She was sure he recognized her too, but he gave all his attention to Mr Leaver, whom he called Mark.

While he was looking round the garden and measuring with an inch tape, Mark Leaver sat down under the apple tree and proceeded to draw on a large sheet of paper which he had brought, attached to a clipboard. Kate went indoors and prepared some coffee for them, and when she returned Mark Leaver showed her a sketch he had drawn of the layout under the apple tree.

'I can supply plants for both places,' he said. 'September is quite a good time for that, but we could wait a bit for the roses.'

While they were speaking, a young girl appeared in the garden. She was about fourteen or fifteen years of age with dark hair, bright eyes. She said to Kate, 'I'm allowed to use the gate between Mrs Paxton and you. She's busy in the kitchen just now. Hello, Garry,' she said, turning to him. 'I haven't seen you for a long time.'

'I go to church every Sunday, but I don't think you can say the same, Miss.' He seemed to speak familiarly to her.

'I know. Daddy gets mad at me, but Mummy says to

leave me alone.' She looked at Kate with what Kate thought great assurance for one so young. 'Mummy says you're not at all like Miss Thom. Much younger, and much prettier.'

'Thank you!' Kate laughed. Her eyes met Mark Leaver's. He was looking up from his board.

'There's praise for you,' he said, smiling.

An elderly woman appeared at the open gate between the two gardens. She smiled at Kate. 'You must be the new tenant. I meant to call. Belle shouldn't have used the gate without getting permission.'

'That's all right,' Kate said. 'You must be Mrs Paxton.'

'Ruth. And you're Kate Armitage – Belle's mother told me. I see you're busy now. Why not come in this afternoon and have a cup of tea?'

Kate hesitated.

'You can direct operations from my kitchen if you're worried. But I can recommend Mark.'

'Thanks, Ruth,' he said.

'And thanks for the invitation,' Kate said. 'What time would you like me to come?'

'About three?'

'That's fine by me.' She smiled at both of them.

'Come along, Belle,' the woman said. Kate saw the girl was talking and laughing with Garry Fox.

She shook her head. 'But I'm enjoying myself, Mrs Paxton! Garry is making me laugh.'

The woman looked at Kate, biting her lip. 'What would you do with a naughty girl?'

'Let her stay,' Kate said. 'Perhaps she could help.'

Belle Dexter clapped her hands. 'See! I'm not in the way.'

'All right. But you must come in when your mother arrives.'

The girl shrugged her shoulders. Mrs Paxton said to Kate, 'Of course, you met Belle's mother?'

36

'Oh, yes. She called on me.' Kate thought the woman's eyes were meaningful.

'Remember, Belle,' she said, 'Mummy will be here soon.'

Belle ignored her.

'See you later.' Mrs Paxton smiled at Kate. 'You can keep an eye on Mark from my kitchen window.' She included him in her smile.

'We'll work away. Don't worry,' he said to Kate, 'we can carry on until five thirty without supervision.'

She offered them sandwiches and coffee at one o'clock, and after tidying up, set off for her appointment with Ruth Paxton.

She wondered if she should use the gate between their gardens, but decided against it, and went out by her front door and wicket gate, then rang the bell next door. She was welcomed with great cordiality by her neighbour and was led into a comfortable sitting room, very like her own, except for the furniture. Every surface was loaded with knick-knacks or photographs.

'Now, I don't think you need to keep an eye on Mark Lever,' Ruth Paxton said, 'but I can't vouch for Garry Fox. Would that chair suit you? You've just missed Barbara Dexter. She called to collect Belle.' She seated herself opposite Kate. 'And how do you like the village so far?' she asked.

'I think I'm going to like it very much. I've just retired, and I've always wanted to get away from London.'

'You look far too young to be retired,' Ruth Paxton smiled at her. She was a buxom woman, her fat knees showed beneath her skirt, which she was tugging at, as if to hide them. Her bright brown eyes reminded Kate of a robin's, as did the position of her head, cocked to one side.

'I'm fifty,' Kate said. Mrs Paxton nodded, as if satisfied.

'The same age as Barbara Dexter. It's no age, now.

Did she tell you about Belle? She usually makes a point of it.'

'No. What do you mean?'

'It's a sad story, but Barbara doesn't want it kept secret. It's Ralph, the vicar, who can't face up to it.' Kate looked at her, her eyebrows raised.

'Unfortunately, when Belle was at the local grammar school she developed epilepsy. She had frequent grand mal seizures, and she's being treated by visits to a specialist in London. Such a blow, and it's Ralph who's taken it badly. Have you noticed that about vicars? Good at solving other people's problems. Do they think they're immune?' She ran on. 'Belle was – well, an afterthought, that's the best way of putting it, seven years younger than the two sons who are very clever . . . well, you can guess . . . They took her away from the grammar school, and at present are waiting for her to obtain a place at a progressive school in Surrey. The doctor feels the seizures may go away as quickly as they came, but it's a trying situation for them all.'

'What a pity,' Kate said. 'She does seem quite . . . bright.' She had been going to say 'precocious' but changed her mind.

'Yes, she is, a typical fifteen-year-old – rebellious. Now, I'm going to bring a tray for us. Come with me and you can look out of my kitchen window and see what they're doing in your garden.'

'All right.' Kate got up, smiling. 'I don't think its necessary, but I'll come and help you, if I may.'

In Mrs Paxton's kitchen, at the window, she said, 'Still beavering away. They've started on the flagging.'

'Mark will keep Garry at it. I knew Mark's wife well, Sheila. Just after they came here she developed cancer, and unfortunately it spread and she died a year after it began. I was the district nurse then. I retired when my husband died, but I still keep an eye on people in the village. Have you heard of our twins, Edna and Eva, in Nettlebed Lane?'

'No, but I've walked up there. It's aptly named.'

'Yes, it is. The twins are seventy-eight now, and most of Nettlebed Lane was their property. Their father, Colonel Blue, sold most of his land to the county council and they built the council houses there. The rest of it was to be their garden, but when he died I'm afraid the twins let it grow wild. Their house is opposite the council ones. Did you notice a gate facing them?'

'No, I don't remember that. But it does look rather derelict – all those nettles. Shall I carry that plate for you? The scones look delicious.'

'Whipped them up after lunch. I hope you like them.'

When they had settled down again in the sitting room, Kate said, 'So Mark Leaver is a widower.' She regretted the remark as soon as she said it, and avoided Mrs Paxton's eye. As if I were a predator, she thought.

'Yes. It was sad. He gave up his job in London – he was an architect – and started up the business here, really for the sake of Sheila. She had green fingers, and always wanted a garden.'

'What a shame!'

'Yes, she was friendly with the twins and intended to help them with their garden. I'm afraid they've deteriorated since then. I used to look in on them quite frequently, and I know Barbara does.'

'You must know most of the village people, because of your job.'

'Oh, yes. At least, one picks up most of the gossip. There is a hard core of the original villagers still. Mostly the men are employed on farms around here and the women in the hospital. The older inhabitants have been here for donkey's years. But I can't say I know many of the incomers. I understand from Barbara that most of the young marrieds who have moved out here have joined the WI – I think singing "Jerusalem" gives them a kick, and they like the crèche for their children. Do I sound mean? I'm afraid I'm a bit churlish about the newcomers. They've changed the character of the village. My husband was the local GP but when he died, no one would take on the practice as it had dwindled. Now we all have to go to Leeston. Changed days. At my age – I'm over sixty now – one resents change, but we must avoid resentment, so I tell myself.'

'I'm beginning to realize that the ideal village, the one that my grandparents lived in, no longer exists. Things have changed.'

'You look to me as if you are perfectly able to cope with that, and of course, for you, being near London here is a great help.'

'Oh, yes, it took me as long to get to my place of work as the train does from here to London.'

'That's the trouble with Edna and Eva Blue. They're in a different world, and I'm afraid far from moving with the times – in fact they've become paranoid. And in a way, this is a forgotten village, being off the beaten track of the motorway. For instance . . .' Lulled by the hot tea and scones, and the bright little fire, Kate half listened. It was obvious that Mrs Paxton was a gossip, not maliciously so, but having been a district nurse she was well-informed.

When Kate got home at around six o'clock, she felt she had had a busy but, on the whole, a non-productive day. She could see that it would be easy to indulge in local gossip with Ruth Paxton, for instance, and allow the time to slip past, but she had to have a project to make her life seem worthwhile. Luckily, she had that in her writing. She had been brought up by her mother to employ her time fruitfully, and remembered how reading during the day had been frowned upon. She would have had the same view on writing.

She started preparing her supper, pleased with the work

that had been accomplished in the garden. There was a note lying on her mat from Mark Leaver, saying that they would be starting at 8.30 a.m. tomorrow.

Five

The following morning Kate found that Mark Leaver was as good as his word. He and Garry Fox were busy laying flags. When she took them their morning coffee, she found that the little pool was filled, and the whole area seemed transformed.

'Garry will carry on,' Mark said to her, 'and I've made out a pattern for the flowers. Are there any you'd particularly like?'

'Old-fashioned ones particularly, and sweet-smelling. Lavender, stocks, pinks, I love their smell, and anything else you think of.'

'I suggest tobacco plants. The smell at night is wonderful – not at all like tobacco! And clematis and honeysuckle for the trellis, and you'll want something for the centre of the pool. You choose. There's a good shop in Leeston, in Old High Street, which has a water features display. Or I thought of water tumbling from above over a series of stones, a little brook, in fact.'

'In Scotland, we call it a burn. If you haven't seen a Highland burn, you haven't lived, but I'll do that. I'll go to Leeston now. I'm quite enthusiastic.'

'Good! If I inspire enthusiasm in my customers, I'm happy.' His mouth quirked. I'd like to see him smile, she thought, then wondered why that should interest her.

When she drove into Leeston soon after, Kate found it busy. She parked in the square under the town clock set in a stone pillar, congratulating herself that she had found an empty space. She noticed an hotel facing the square, and decided to have a sandwich and a coffee there before she started on a tour of Leeston. It was busy, dark and the pub noise greeting her made her think of London pubs, everyone talking, laughing, waiters darting about. She was directed to an empty table, too large for her, and had no sooner sat down than a smartly-dressed young woman with a small boy in tow stopped at the table. 'I see this is the only empty space. Do you mind if we sit here?'

'Not at all,' Kate smiled. 'It's too big for me.'

The lady helped the little boy on to a chair. 'Now, Seb,' she said, 'sit nicely, and Mummy will get you a drink with a straw. Won't that be nice?'

'Lady,' the little boy said, pointing at Kate. He was an adorable child, she thought, a proper little man, and dressed like one in jeans, a checked shirt and pullover, with a minute leather jacket on top.

'Thanks for the compliment.' She smiled at the girl. 'He's a lovely child. What age is he?'

'Three and a bit. Precocious.'

The waiter had appeared, and Kate ordered sandwiches and a coffee for herself. The girl asked for coffee and cranberry juice with a straw for the little boy.

'I'm trying to keep him off pseudo-orange,' she said. 'I suppose I'll have to give in when he goes to school. Where we live has only an infant school. Roger, my husband, is all in favour of the grammar school later, but that means passing the entry exam. It becomes very difficult. I don't know much about it. I was at boarding school.'

'I suppose it must be,' Kate said. 'My mother had no choice. I was at grammar school, or an academy as we called them in Scotland.' She remembered being imprisoned at the kitchen table, books all over it and her grim-faced mother going about her duties, glancing at her from time to time.

'Oh, the education is much better there, I believe.'

43

Kate shrugged. 'I wouldn't know. It won't concern me, as I don't have any children. I've just moved to Mellor from London.'

'So have we!' The girl was excited. 'We discovered it quite by chance, then saw that some enterprising builder had got there before us. We're in Lansdown Lane. Roger drives up to town every day. I find it rather quiet.'

'Me too. But you've got everything going for you, there are a lot of young people with children, I believe, and I have it on excellent authority that the WI has a crèche. Have you tried it?'

'No, I haven't.'

'Finished, Mummy.' The little boy banged his glass on the table.

'All right, Seb.' She wiped his mouth with her paper napkin. 'I've promised him a visit to Woolworth's, which he dearly loves, so I'd better get going.' She finished her coffee, then took the boy on her knee and started wrestling him into his jacket. 'My name's Lorna Crook. Where do you live in the village?'

'I'm Kate Armitage. In the cottages facing the Green. Rose Cottage. There are two climbing roses round the door, a pink and a white. I'm not good at names, unfortunately, but I shall have to learn.'

'Perhaps we'll meet in the local post office.'

'Perhaps. Or the WI.'

What a pretty girl, Kate thought, as Lorna Crook disappeared with her son in tow. She'll soon find people like herself in the village. In her own case, it would be more difficult. I hope there's someone between Barbara Dexter and Ruth Paxton. Not being married hadn't mattered in London, there was such a variety of relationships. Would she end up by doing good works? But there's my book, she reminded herself. That places me in a different category.

She walked round Leeston, and eventually found the shop Mark Leaver had mentioned in a narrow street leading to the cathedral. There were several water features on show, and she saw one she liked, a series of stones set in a frame. She lifted a brochure from the display, and to show willing, bought a cast iron stork with down-bent head, which appealed to her. She hoped it would appeal to Mark Leaver. She found other shops that interested her, principally delicatessens. That was a bonus, she thought. They're probably catering for people like me who feel marooned if they can't indulge their taste for exotica in food. On the whole, Leeston gave her the impression of having been updated. The streets leading off the square were narrow and cobbled, and the shop fronts there were definitely not twentieth century.

She drove back and found Mark Leaver on the point of going home. She showed him the brochures she had collected, and indicated the one she liked. 'Yes, we could adapt that,' he said. 'Or better still, I could copy it. I have stones at home. And I like your bird,' he said when she showed it to him. 'We'll have to think of a name for him.'

'Percy?' she said. He laughed, and she saw his smile. Gratifying, she thought, like the pleasure one gets on a dark day, when suddenly there is a glimpse of sun.

'I'll come tomorrow and plant up,' he said, 'and then all we have to do is give everything a final watering. Are you pleased with the flagging?'

'Yes, it's nice. He seems to be a good worker, Garry Fox.'

'He is. Some people in the village don't like him, but I have no complaints. Well, I'll get going. Tomorrow should see the job finished.'

'Good,' she said. 'I'm very pleased.'

She pondered about Mark Leaver when she was having her supper. What is it that I find appealing? she asked herself. She thought back to Gavin, and remembered how she had grown to love him very quickly. Certainly they had been thrown together, but for her it had been her first love, a tremulous feeling, a longing to be with him, and how he was constantly in her thoughts. Unlike John Newton and the feeling of impermanency she always felt with him, as if each visit would be his last. She had always felt she didn't add to his life, except in a physical sense. Her gradual giving in had been against her better judgement. To have a partner in love, to assuage one's natural feelings, had seemed right for her, as long as she reminded herself it could never be more than that. This puzzle about herself still existed. Was that why she wanted to explore her father's life? She knew her mother. She had lived with her for eighteen years, had never known freedom until she came to London and was her own woman, for better or for worse. There she had relied on her own judgement, and had given that impression, as she well knew.

The following day Kate went upstairs to her computer. She had thought that the novel would flow easily, but she had to struggle, and chop and change before she got going again.

The eternal triangle, she thought. Now she had a possible explanation for her mother's character. And then, perhaps she had really loved George, and thought perhaps he would marry her when her husband died. Her marriage to Robert had not been happy. By all accounts she was a bright, vivacious girl, very different from the embittered woman Kate had known. It seemed the mystery had been solved, and that perhaps the answer lay in the genes. But what chance did that give Kate of finding happiness?

Isobel and Anne were strolling by the river. Isobel had found it difficult to resist Anne when she had called that morning. She was so beguiling. 'Oh, good, you're alone, Isobel. Are the boys out?'

'Yes.' She wasn't going to be taken in by her friend's charms. 'They've gone to the cattle market together.'

'Good. I thought you and I might have a walk and a chat together, the way we used to do.'

'I thought you hadn't time for me, now there are two men about the house?'

'Oh, Isobel, how can you say that! I enjoy teasing them but they don't mean anything to me, except that they are your brothers.'

'At one time I thought you hadn't ideas for anyone but George.'

She saw the girl's eyes flicker. 'I don't know what you mean. George and I will always be good friends, Robert too. Maybe you don't like me teasing them so much, is that it? You don't know how lucky you are. You had a father and a mother and two brothers. I know your parents died, but at least you've got George and now Robert. Our house is so dull with just Mrs Collins and my father in Glasgow most of the time.'

'I know, Anne. It must be miserable for you at times. Do you never go to see your mother?'

'No, Dad doesn't think it wise. Or at least the owners of the home where she is think it would be unwise.'

47

'*What's wrong with her?*' *Isobel had never asked this question before.*

'*It's an incurable disease.*' *Anne's face was pitiful.* '*She requires constant nursing.*' *It sounded to Isobel almost rehearsed, as though she was repeating what she had been told to say.* '*I've valued your friendship very much, Isobel. Most of my school friends have left the village. I get so lonely and depressed, and your house is like . . . a beacon of light.*'

'*I'm glad.*' *Why does this not ring true to me? she thought. Anne was speaking like one schoolgirl to another, but what about that afternoon when Anne had been upstairs, and so had George? And her strange eyes? She and Anne were both twenty-one now, capable of affairs, although she herself had never had one. But it was a dead-and-alive village. Had she not been tied up with nursing both parents in their last illnesses, and then running the house for George and Robert, Isobel would have been able to get around more, meet people.*

And yet, you had to pity Anne. She decided to be light in what she said. '*I'm glad you like coming around, Anne, and we've been good friends. Just leave George and Robert out of it, or you'll have them tearing each other's hair out.*'

'*That's the last thing I want to happen.*' *They were walking along the towpath. The river was shallow here and huge boulders jutted out of the water.*

'*Look at these great stones!*' *Isobel said.* '*Have you ever wondered why they're there?*'

'*Yes. I can just see Stone Age men wandering about here. Maybe they wanted to dam the river, or they collected large stones to be broken up for building a bridge. I can just see them in their fur jackets shambling about . . .*'

'*What an imagination you have!*'

'Yes, my mind goes skittering about, especially when I'm in bed . . .'

'What a funny girl you are. You quite frighten me at times!'

'Do I? Do you think I frighten your brothers?'

'I wouldn't know. But I think most men are interested in how a girl looks, not what her character is like.'

'I sometimes think I'm different from most girls. I see the effect I have on them, and the look of fear in their eyes.'

'What a strange thing to say! I never think of the effect I have on people. I'm me, and they can take it or leave it.'

'It must be good to feel like that, so sure of yourself . . .' Anne looked at her watch. 'I must get back. Mrs Collins is going shopping to Glasgow, and we're having an early lunch. Perhaps I'll look in at your place in the afternoon and say hello to George and Robert. Is that all right with you?'

'Suit yourself.' Isobel wasn't going to encourage her. She had an uneasy feeling that anything to do with Anne Kay meant trouble, a feeling that trouble was brewing. It didn't take long to happen.

A week later George and Robert were returning from a visit to Lord Belmorris. He had heard Robert was back from Burma, and asked them to visit. The old lord was sitting in his wheelchair in the window overlooking the river. The view was splendid. 'I can see all my territory from here,' he joked, with a laughing wheeze, his little white moustache going up and down. The butler, James, had come in bearing a tray. 'I like tea and lemon at this time. I've kept up my wife's practise.' He watched while the butler dispensed tea. 'That's fine, James. The far field looks good, George. You're letting it lie fallow, this year?'

'Yes, my lord. We were thinking it might be a good idea to put Robert's cattle in there for a term. It's a fine, sunny field and they're due to calve quite soon.'

Lord Belmorris looked at Robert. 'It's a good idea?'

'Yes, sir. I'm in touch with a breeder in the North, and he's giving me a few tips.'

'Good. You should always take advice from someone who knows better than you. But you'd have learnt that in the army.'

'Yes, sir. But I'm glad to be back, although I'll probably move around a bit.'

'George,' Lord Belmorris looked at him, 'when your father bought the farm from me, I know it was with a view to leaving it to you, the elder son but – forgive me if I'm treading where I shouldn't – what about Robert?'

Robert threw a glance at George. 'Let me answer, sir. My father left me a sum of money. It was on the understanding that I could either buy my way into the farm with George or take the money and run. Of course he wasn't sure that I would return from the war. We have a few points to consider first.'

Lord Belmorris tut-tutted. 'If you'll forgive me saying so, your father was no businessman. But I've interfered quite enough. Nevertheless I'd be interested to know what you decide, Robert. It may not be my land any more but the Armitages have looked after it for over a hundred years, and I shouldn't like to see any changes to what has been an admirable arrangement.'

They took the towpath home after having been shown out by James, whom they knew well as he was a village lad. 'Nice to see you both together again,' he said to them on the steps.

They strode along, not speaking, looking straight ahead. It was George who began at last. 'I don't like our dirty linen being washed in public.'

'*You can't blame the old codger. It used to be his land until quite recently, he's bound to be interested.*'

'*I can see that. He's astute. He's guessed that there's something going on.*'

'*Well, you know the situation.*'

'*I know the situation, but it has changed since Father's will.*'

'*Would you like me to go off then, and keep the money?*'

'*I can't trust you.*'

'*You mean, I might take Anne with me?*'

'*Maybe it's her I don't trust.*'

'*I don't think she had any cause to trust you either. Oh, I know you, George. You were always the same. Fun but no commitment.*'

'*I resent that.*' George stopped and faced Robert. '*Repeat that insinuation, if you dare.*' They were facing each other. Robert was smiling.

'*Certainly. She was your mistress. You kept putting her off—*' George's fist smashed into Robert's face so that he toppled from his feet, staggered over the towpath and fell into the river. The current was fast, and he would have been swept away had George not rushed to grasp his waving arm. He pulled him out, and they faced each other, both panting.

Robert said, a slight smile on his face, '*That was silly. I could have drowned.*'

'*Well, I pulled you out, didn't I?*'

'*You want me to thank you? Don't forget you pushed me in.*'

'*I'm sorry. But you and I were always good friends, weren't we?*'

'*A lot of water has flowed under the bridge since then.*'

They stood, staring at each other, panting, then Robert said, throwing an arm round George's shoulders, '*Come*

51

on then, we'll get home. Isobel will be wondering where
we've got to. Besides, I'm shivering. I'll have to change.'
  'You slip upstairs while I'm talking to her. I've
apologized to you. I'll tell her we were mucking about
at the side of the Morris, and you slipped and fell in.'
  'OK.'
  'Marching along, along . . .' he sang, his arm still
round George's shoulders.
  George joined in. 'No woman's worth it,' he said.
'It takes more than that to come between us.'
  Robert didn't reply. When they reached the house
he slipped upstairs, changed his clothes, and put the
wet ones in the linen basket in the bathroom. Isobel
was no fool. She'd put two and two together.
  Then there was Anne. She wanted him to take her
away from the village and George. He thought he loved
her, and yet . . . there was something odd abut her that
made him feel uneasy. Those eyes . . .
  *George and I are stupid to let her come between
us, he thought. She was captivating, playing one
brother against the other, charming him, influencing
him. He'd much prefer to use the money to buy himself
into the farm with George, but he was in the grip of
his passion for Anne. When he was with her, he forgot
everything.*

Six

Kate began to enjoy the book, it was like solving a jigsaw puzzle. She had to build the village from scraps of information and fleeting memories. She knew, from visits to her grandfather on her mother's side, what it was like. She remembered the long road leading to it, the wall that ran alongside it, which enclosed the grounds of Manor Farm. She remembered scuffling her feet in the autumn leaves that had gathered at the foot of the wall. She remembered the river, and the steep road leading down to it, and her grandfather taking her for a walk there, sucking the 'lollipop' he had made for her, a cut stalk of rhubarb, peeled of its pink skin, which she dipped into the small bag of sugar he had given her.

'I used to know Manor Farm very well,' her mother had once said as they walked beside the wall. 'Your uncle George lived there. He was wealthy, but lazy. Your father could have run it better than him. George was nice . . .' When Kate looked at her, her face had a faraway look. 'He died after we went to Glasgow,' she was saying. 'Now Isobel runs the farm. It might have been me.'

'Couldn't we visit her?' Kate remembered asking, and her mother's tight-lipped expression, that face which had covered so many secrets.

'No, certainly not. If they could forget your father, they aren't worth visiting.'

Once Kate stopped recollecting her parents' village in Scotland and was concentrating on Glasgow, she felt the book was rolling along, almost without her help. She remembered the small flat they had lived in near the Clyde, and jaunts they made across the Clyde on the ferry to visit friends, and what an adventure that had been, watching the cars drive on, then ordered into neat rows and the gates swinging shut, the disembarking at the other side with the Clyde water swishing over their wheels at the exit. A new world, Renfrew. She remembered departure from that flat, and the pleasure on her mother's face as she and Margaret had packed china, and being allowed to help, wrapping her dolls in sheets torn from the *Herald*. 'Going up in the world,' her mother had called it, 'as good as Manor Farm.'

Then the house in Kelvinside where she grew up, clear in her memory. As were her mother, her sister and brother. Schooldays, Margaret and Robert being hurried in the morning to catch the bus to school, resplendent in their school uniform. Her mother using her as a confidante.

'They want to bring their school friends here, but I don't see why I should let them. I never invite the neighbours over. It's just nosiness on their part, dying to see inside the house. That's why they were all so nice when your daddy died, to get in, to poke their noses in.'

Kate, as the youngest child, had begun to believe that outside the house, enemies lurked. You had to barricade the doors against them. To begin with there was much petting of the little sister by her elder brother and sister, but as time went on and they were at those 'big' schools, they hadn't time for her; Margaret and Roy were always with their friends. There were jokes between them that she didn't understand. It was better to be with Mother, to be like her.

Kate remembered sitting in the parlour on the green rug, and listening to the voices of Margaret and Mary, their young maid, an Irish girl from a poor home, wise beyond her years. Kate remembered her being despatched summarily, because she had been thieving.

'Do you mean to say you don't *know*?' Mary was saying.

She was rubbing with metal polish the chandelier that hung from the centre of the ceiling. Margaret's face was raised to Mary, who had clambered down the steps to put her mouth to Margaret's ear. She had watched Margaret's face swelling up and getting redder and redder. Just before it exploded, she had burst out with words Kate didn't know. 'That's filthy, Mary!' Listening again as her face grew paler and paler. 'But I thought Mrs Lennox was just growing fatter!' And Mary's triumphant face, pointing to Kate, 'How do you think *she* arrived!'

She remembered Mr Bannister who came to see her mother when Daddy had died, and how once he brought a tiny dog, a Pekinese, as a present. And liking to have Chinky on her lap and stroke her golden fur. And how one day she had gone to the shops for her mother, and on the way a nasty terrier had followed her, jumping up on her, barking and snapping. And how people had smiled. She hadn't been able to shake it off. It had followed her into the shop and back to the house again. All her mother had said was, 'Don't take Chinky on your lap again.' She remembered Mother and Mr Bannister going into the front room with the oriel window and Mother saying, 'You haven't to come in. Get on with your lessons. I have to show Mr Bannister something.'

Then there were the endless fittings, also in the parlour, of the dresses her mother made for her. 'Stand still! What's the point of me working my fingers to the bone, picking up remnants, sewing away, when you can't even stand still? I wouldn't have to do this if your father hadn't died, and that deputy of his ruined the business, after Daddy had sunk all his inheritance in it.' How Kate had envied girls at parties with bought dresses from one of the big stores in Sauchiehall Street.

Her schooldays had slid by. She worked well, was attentive and docile. The conditions at home seemed to be fraught. Margaret was in constant trouble with their mother for coming in late. All Kate remembered was her mother shouting abuse at her, ending with, 'If the cap fits, wear it!' She couldn't understand it, but she wakened in the middle of the night to Margaret's muffled sobbing . . . Then it seemed she was being dressed up as Margaret's bridesmaid, and Margaret was standing beside James Stewart, whom Mother didn't like, and being married. Late that night, she listened to her mother's dirge. 'That's all the thanks I get, left alone with no money to bring up three children, and being spurned by them!' She had put an arm round her mother's shoulders but her mother had shaken it away.

Then Roy was going off to university, and he appeared home later with Karin, a bright girl whom her mother also didn't like, then the terrible time at home with her mother when his letter came, saying that he was living in Leeds, he had got a job there and was getting married to Karin. She and her mother didn't go to that wedding. Perhaps they weren't asked.

Kate was deeply envious of Roy, not for getting married, but for being able to go to university. Mother said girls didn't need a university education; a business or nursing qualification was more suitable for them. She remembered the dullness of the business college, of getting a job on the *Reporter* and meeting Gavin.

Life changed for her then. Girl friends had been few and far between because Mother didn't want them in the house. She had Gavin. A boyfriend. Much better than a girl friend. Mother didn't approve of her relationship with Gavin. 'You're just going to be like the other two. Can't wait to get away and leave me alone.' And then the refrain, 'Work my fingers to the bone . . . that's all the thanks I get . . .' That was when Kate began to apply for jobs in London, keeping it secret.

Around this time Kate and her mother went on holiday to the Clyde Coast, and while they were there her mother scanned the Glasgow papers, saying that Kate was underpaid at the *Reporter*, and she shouldn't go back. Kate's cheeks burned at the recollection because she had followed her mother's advice, applied for a job in a city office and got it. It was a peculiar thing, she thought, that if she applied for a job she always got it. Employers seemed to like her. She had wept in bed at her stupidity, especially as Gavin told her that she had 'blotted her copybook' with the *Reporter* for leaving so abruptly and it was a stupid thing to do.

'I'm the only one who stood up for you,' he had said.

'Why did you?' It was then that she realized she would have to get away from her mother's influence. But marrying Gavin wasn't the answer. She would try to get a job in London and make a fresh start. Something had gone wrong with her. Perhaps it was because she had had no father, and her mother had had the whip hand and she had been brainwashed. This occurred to her now.

She had told Margaret about it on the telephone, who by now had a baby, and Margaret had said, 'Don't blame yourself. I know what she's like. Constant water wearing away stone. Get away!' Which she did, to London, and the publishing firm. Her mother's rage was frightening, as was the hysterical weeping. She had to steel herself. 'Just like the other two,' she had said. 'You work your fingers to the bone and what thanks do you get?'

She had been sad to lose Gavin, but life in London soon compensated for that.

When Kate read what she had typed she thought, No one will understand this. How a malleable girl can be worked upon, her constant feeling of resentment against her mother. And how afraid of her she had been, mixed with pity. Margaret had been right.

The only one who could make her mother smile was Mr Bannister. On one of his visits after she had been widowed he left a box of chocolate biscuits – Jaffa Cakes they were called, sponge, then an orange jelly on top of that, sealed with a chocolate topping. Kate became adept at prising off the lid and stealing one, of wearing an innocent face when her mother said, 'These biscuits that Mr Bannister brought have gone down at a rate.' She could have said truthfully, 'It's surprising, because we never have anyone here for tea . . .' But anything connected with Mr Bannister seemed to have a soothing effect. Mother would laugh girlishly, and for a time after his visit continue to wear the orange lipstick that sometimes smeared her teeth. Kate would have liked to tell her, but the lipstick was a secret, and was never mentioned.

Sometimes Kate felt she wasn't writing about her father, but more of her mother, and how her influence had poisoned all the family. She decided she would leave the book to simmer for a time.

It was like emerging from a deep, stagnant pool, and looking around at the countryside. On one of these occasions, Kate thought she would walk to the vicarage, past the duck pond. Perhaps she would call, perhaps she would walk past. She would see how she felt.

She set off, but when she reached the village hall, she heard 'Jerusalem' being rendered by strong female voices, then there was a clatter of chairs, and the door was flung open as women and children began to emerge. She was just going to move on when she saw Barbara Dexter standing in the doorway, smiling and speaking to those around her. Her eyes fell on Kate, and she waved and came towards her. 'Kate! I'm so glad to see you. You should have been at our meeting today! Would you like to walk with me to the vicarage and we could have a chat?'

'As a matter of fact,' Kate said, 'I had every intention of calling on you today. I've been rather busy recently.'

'Come along, then. Oh, here's Lorna!' It was the girl whom Kate had met in Leeston. She had her little boy with her.

'We've already met,' the girl said. 'Say hello, Seb.'

'Don't bother him,' Kate smiled at the child. If she'd had one, she would have liked a little boy like Seb, with his grown-up clothes.

'I'm so glad to have seen you,' Lorna Crook said. 'Look, would you come for tea tomorrow? And you too, Mrs Dexter?'

'Sorry,' Barbara said. 'That's the day I visit the twins, Edna and Eva. They're practically in their eighties, and if I rearranged I think it would upset them.'

'Oh, I've heard of them,' Lorna Crook said. 'Someone told me they've lived here all their lives.'

'Yes, you're quite right.'

This is very unlike London, Kate thought, listening to the exchange. Tea, WI, village characters. Have I fallen into a time warp?

'How romantic!' The girl had a lovely smile. She could be my daughter. 'Well, will you come, Kate? I'm so glad to run into you again.'

'I'd love to,' she said. 'What time?'

'Around four o'clock?'

'Right! See you then.'

'We'll start walking, then,' Barbara said. 'Do come next month, Lorna. You'll make lots of friends, I'm sure.'

It was pleasant walking with Barbara Dexter. They chatted easily, and from time to time they met people whom Barbara always greeted with her bright smile. Sometimes she introduced Kate, sometimes not. 'Is it difficult being friendly with everyone?' Kate asked her.

'It was at first. I'm really very shy. I wish I were like you. You have such a sophisticated air, so sure of yourself. Maybe living in London gives one that.'

Kate was astonished. 'That doesn't sound like me at all. I had an . . . overbearing mother, and I was not at all sure of myself when I lived with her. I made all kinds of mistakes, because I was never allowed to exercise my own judgement.'

'It doesn't follow. My mother was the typical vicar's wife. She's still alive, organizing everybody, now that she hasn't my father to organize. He died three years ago. I still miss him.' Her face grew sad. 'I scarcely knew mine. He died when I was very young.' 'How sad for you!' The face Barbara turned to her was full of concern. 'My father taught me so much, not merely by example.'

They had reached the vicarage. Kate said, 'I'll leave you here.'

'Not at all,' Barbara said immediately. 'You must come in and meet Ralph, and Belle. But I hear you met her at Ruth Paxton's. Ruth has been very helpful to me. Belle has epilepsy, you know.'

'Yes, Mrs Paxton told me. I believe you're waiting to get her to a progressive school?'

'They're taking a long time. Belle needs strong discipline. I'm pretty good at that, but Ralph isn't.'

They had walked round the back of the house while they were talking and Barbara led Kate through a large kitchen into an equally large, untidy room. 'Hello, there!' Barbara said. Belle, and presumably her father, were sitting at a small table in the window, which looked on to an untidy looking garden. There was a chessboard between them.

'Hello, darling,' the man said in reply, smiling uncertainly at Kate.

'This is Kate Armitage, Ralph. I told you about her.' He rose to shake hands with Kate.

'And how do you like the village, Miss Armitage?' he said.

'I like it,' she said. 'Please call me Kate.'

Belle Dexter was on her feet. 'Hello,' she said. 'Do I call you Kate?'

Kate laughed, looking at her parents. 'Anything's better than Miss Armitage.'

'I met Kate at Mrs Paxton's,' Belle said. 'Garry Fox was working in her garden. He makes me laugh.'

'Well, see if you can make Kate laugh,' Barbara said, 'while I make some tea.'

'Please,' Kate said, 'not on my account.'

'Ralph would be very disappointed if you didn't stay. Tea is his favourite meal.'

'That's true,' he said. 'And Barbara panders to my old-fashioned tastes.' He turned to Kate, 'I believe you've come from London?'

'Yes, but originally Scotland. But I went south, along with millions of Scots.'

'Yes, there's been an invasion. I notice their voices around, mostly on radio.'

When they had finished tea, which was very substantial with scones and cakes, Belle said, 'I could walk you home, Kate.' She seemed eager to leave the house.

'No, Belle,' her father said, 'you know you have your piano lesson today.'

'Oh, Daddy!' she pouted.

'I don't blame her,' Ralph Dexter said to Kate. 'I'm her teacher.'

'He plays the violin with me,' Belle said, still scowling.

'Well, you shouldn't miss that,' Kate said. 'But I'm willing to have a walk with you any time. Just give me a ring.'

When she got home, Kate went upstairs to her study. Her talk with Barbara Dexter had made her think. Barbara had spoken warmly of her own father. It had struck Kate as she listened that she herself hadn't been able to write anything positive about *her* father. She sat in front of the computer, thinking hard, and then it came to her, complete, like a scene in a play.

Once, when she was a child, before he died, Kate had been wakened by sobbing, loud sobbing, coming from her parents' bedroom. Margaret was sitting up in bed. 'What's that?' she had asked, afraid.

61

'I think it's Mother,' Margaret said. 'Lie down.'

Roy came into their room in pyjamas. 'Is she ill?' he asked.

'I don't know,' Margaret said. She put her legs over the bed. 'I'm going to see.' She ran to the door, which Roy had left open, and was gone. Roy looked at Kate. 'You'd better stay here.' He was at the door, listening. The dreadful sobbing continued, making the hairs stand up on the back of Kate's neck. Then Roy was gone.

Kate sat for a second or two, then she heard her father's voice. She remembered thinking, Poor Daddy, and then she too was running along the corridor, as fast as her little legs would carry her. When she got to her parents' bedroom, she saw Roy and Margaret were standing at the door, looking in.

'What's wrong with her, Daddy?' Margaret said.

Kate looked in and saw her mother sitting in a basket chair with her hands over her face. Her sobbing wasn't so loud now. Father was bent over her. 'Come on now, Anne,' he was saying. 'Come back to bed. See how you've upset the children.' She was shaking her head, pulling away.

'I didn't want to leave George,' she said. 'You made me.'

Kate saw her father's agonized face raised to theirs. 'Off you three go, and I'll make a cup of tea for Mother. She'll settle down.'

They trailed back to their bedrooms. Roy didn't speak. Margaret's face was angry. 'She gives him a terrible time,' she said. It was such a grown-up thing to say, Kate thought now.

The next day was Saturday. Mother was busy at her sewing machine. Father took them all to buy cakes and candles, swags of silver trimming. When they got back, Mother had finished sewing and was getting ready, Father said. He helped them to dress, Roy in his best suit, Margaret in her party dress, then mother appeared with a white tulle dress with a full skirt and a satin bodice made for Kate, and a wand with a silver star at the end. Kate remembered her eyes were strange, shining. Robert went off with Father to set up Dobbin the rocking horse, in the front room, while Margaret and Mother helped Kate to dress. There was a large cupboard in the room with curtains in front of it instead of a door, and Dobbin was in the cupboard. Mother and Father sat down after setting up the old gramophone with some equally old dance tunes.

Margaret helped Kate on to the back of the horse and gave her the wand to hold, then Roy pulled back the curtains to reveal Kate balanced on Dobbin's back, waving her wand. Mother and Father clapped, and Roy and Margaret bowed. Then Mother and Father got up and danced, and he swung her round while the gramophone played the Blue Danube. 'Come on, children,' Daddy had said, 'we're having a party for Mother!' When they had finished dancing, Mother brought in some lovely cakes and drinks on a tray, and they all laughed and sang to the music. It was a lovely time and it had been buried deep in Kate's memory. 'Was my little girl happy?' Father asked her, putting an arm round her shoulders.

Now she saw that the party had been designed by Father to make them forget Mother's crying, but nothing would ever make Kate forget that. Then father died. He got pneumonia by standing in the foundry supervising the men, then going out into the cold yard. He could have been cured of the pneumonia, but his heart was damaged, and he died suddenly. Margaret said it had been terrible and Mother had cried and cried, and said it was her fault. Then she got so difficult that as fast as they could she and Roy left home to be married. The rest Kate knew. It all went into her book.

On the day she was due to visit Lorna Crook for tea, Kate dressed carefully. Barbara Dexter had said she looked sophisticated, but she wanted to look casual. It was too cold for new summer dresses – it was now the end of October – so she wore a favourite black dress, and on top of it a soft pink cardigan. She intended to walk there, so that she would have an excuse to leave before dark, and she put on black sandals with low heels. She did her hair up on top of her head. It was perhaps too sophisticated, but Lorna wore hers loose and Kate felt she should look her age.

Lorna welcomed her at the glass front door and led her through a conservatory to the sitting room. The little boy was there too.

'Lady,' he said.

'Hello, Seb,' Kate said. 'That's a lovely barrow you have.'

'I'm loading it,' he said. He sat down on the carpet beside a pile of toys.

'Kate doesn't want to play,' his mother said. 'Well, one thing.' He was holding out a brick to Kate.

'Just one, Seb,' Kate said. 'Now I'm going to talk to Mummy.'

Lorna drew her to a window seat. 'Don't get embroiled,' she said to Kate. 'They would suck your blood.' Kate gave her a look.

'That's a granny look,' Lorna said. 'I don't mean you look like a granny, but it's still the look.'

'Sorry,' Kate smiled at her. 'I suppose I'm a bit of a romantic about children. For instance, I could run away with your Seb, but then I wouldn't know what to do with him.'

'You're like Roger. He comes home ready to play and pet Seb like a favourite toy, and he doesn't give him the benefit of recognizing that he's a growing child, sometimes bad, manipulative, or his own self. Obviously Roger makes him feel good, but he also makes him the reverse. He stifles him.'

'Are you resentful of having a child?' Kate asked.

Lorna looked at her. 'You're clever as well as beautiful. Yes, I am a bit resentful. But I can come back to what I was doing, which was making pots. I'm hoping to set up a kiln here in a few years and get going . . . unless Roger cons me into having another baby. I mustn't put it all on to Roger. I also want children. And I want to make a good job of it.'

'My growing up wasn't so carefully considered. My father died and left my mother with three children, and she couldn't cope. There was a sister and a brother as well as me.'

'What age would your mother be when your father died?'

'Oh, a young woman.'

'And attractive?'

Kate thought of the Anne Kay whom Cathy Livingstone had described. 'Yes,' she said, 'from all accounts.' And then there was Mr Bannister, she thought.

'I should be devastated if I lost Roger, or if he decided to leave me. I need him. You'll understand that, Kate. Now, my mother is different. Fortunately, my father is alive, and they bill and coo quite happily together, as befits their age, but they are an item; she would be lost without him.'

'Lady!' Seb said imperiously. 'I need more bricks.'

'OK,' Kate said, jumping up. She caressed his tender nape as she knelt beside him, looking down, appreciating how his hair curled on its soft whiteness.

'I'll let you play with him while I fetch tea,' his mother said.

'Right. I shall be going fairly soon. It's dark quite early.'

'Didn't you drive down?'

'No, I have to get exercise. I must guard against embonpoint at my age.'

'I don't think that's going to be a problem with you. Well, we'll get you home. I should have told you, but Roger's coming early tonight because I've invited my next-door neighbour, Mark Leaver, for drinks.'

'I've met him. He's done some work on my garden for me. I want it spick and span for next year.'

'He always looks so sad to me. And he works like mad in those greenhouses.'

'I believe his wife died just after he came here.'

'Oh, well I'm glad I invited him.'

Kate felt thoroughly at home with the girl and her son. Seb sat on her knee and went to sleep, and he was there when his father came in. He's just as I thought he would be, Kate thought, watching him kiss his wife and put his hand on the child's head. 'He's made himself at home, then,' he said.

'This is Kate, darling,' Lorna said. 'She's escaped from London, just like us.'

'I've retired here.' Kate smiled at him. Very pleasing to the eye, she thought,

'Good for you. I wouldn't mind doing that. I'd like to get going on the garden here.'

'He knows all the Latin names too,' Lorna said. 'Would you like some tea, after your hard day in the city, sweetheart?' She looked teasingly at him.

'No, thanks. I must go and get some bottles out. Did Lorna tell you we had asked our neighbour in?' he said to Kate.

'Yes, but since I walked here I may have to leave soon.'

'I'll take you home. You must stay.'

When Mark Leaver arrived, Lorna greeted him, saying, 'Kate tells me you two have met?'

'Indeed we have.' Seb woke up and jumped off Kate's knee.

'Man,' he said, he was at Mark's knee holding out a brick.

'He's very demanding,' Roger said. 'Ignore him.'

'Impossible,' Mark said. 'He's a sweetie.' He took the brick, got up and dropped it in the barrow. 'There you are, Seb,' he smiled at the little boy.

'Lorna really doesn't get time for her work,' Roger said. Henpecked, Kate thought, then silently chastised herself. 'But she's setting up a studio. She's raring to go.'

'Potting?' Mark Leaver said, then turned to Kate. 'If you haven't any hobbies – what a hateful word that is – I'm looking for an assistant in the greenhouses.'

'No, thank you. I shall be pretty busy.' Does that sound as if I've taken umbrage? she thought, and decided to come clean. 'I write.'

'Oh, do you?' Lorna said. 'You lucky thing. I'm a hands-on person. I can scarcely write a postcard.'

'Well, you can pot,' Kate said. '"Handless" my mother called me, so I lived up to it.'

'I think circumstances alter cases,' Mark Leaver said. 'Look at me. Sheila, my wife, she died a year ago, was the one with green fingers. I took on her job, which essentially is composed of sticking things into pots. But I had to read it up. And now I'm managing to run the place.'

'What was your job?' Roger asked.

'I was an architect. We came here for Sheila's sake.'

Watching his face, Kate had the impression that he was making himself talk about his wife. 'Well,' she said, 'your eye had been developed before. I'm sure that will help you. Look how you drew a plan for my garden!'

'Garry Fox could have done it without me,' he said.

'But there has to be a boss,' Roger said, 'one who carries the can and takes the blame. I'm intrigued about your writing, Kate. Had you done much before? Should I know you?'

'Only if you read romantic novels.' They all laughed. 'It was a fluke, really, I happened to write one that was a success, now I'm searching my soul, as a friend advised me to do.' My lover, she thought. I wonder what these nice people would say if I were to come out with that?

There was a pause. She looked out at the garden, it was dusk, the trees black shadows. Quiet. It had fallen silent, the way it never did in London, expect for a few hours in the early morning. The four of them talked amicably for quite a long time, but when Seb was taken away by his mother for bed, Kate said, 'I think I should be on my way too.' She laughed. 'I realize this isn't London. I can't call a taxi.'

67

'I'll take you,' Roger said, 'if you must.'

'No,' Mark Leaver was on his feet. 'My car is at the front of my house. I could take you home, Kate.'

'What a fuss! I'll never come without a car again. I'm sorry.'

Roger looked from one to the other. 'Well, if you must go, Kate, and Mark is determined to squire you, that's it settled. But you both must come again.'

Lorna had come into the room. 'Yes, you must,' she said, 'but for dinner next time. I'm not much of a cook, but I'd love to have you.'

They moved to the door, talking, and then Kate and Mark were walking towards his car. 'I feel this looks like a put-up job,' she said.

'On whose part?'

'First of all, me not driving.'

'And perhaps Lorna thinking there's two people who might get on together.'

'No, I don't think her mind works that way.'

'Well, it must be you.'

'No, I'm exonerated. I was invited for tea only. I thought a country walk was quite on the cards.'

They were in the car now, and speeding up the lane. The Hare and Hounds was brightly lit.

'If it weren't for the fact that I'm liable to be stopped for drinking and driving I would offer you another drink,' Mark said.

'And I should refuse, although I doubt if the village bobby is out and about.'

'Shall we risk it?'

Kate shook her head. 'No thanks. I'm not desperate for a drink in any case.'

'Neither am I. Gosh, we've arrived!'

'Well, thanks very much, Mr Leaver,' Kate said. She got out of the car.

'Mark, please.' He was beside her on the pavement. There

was, to Kate, an uncomfortable pause. They stood, Kate waiting for him to speak, he doubtless for her.

'Well, goodnight,' she said, holding out her hand. 'Thanks for the lift.'

He shook it, then opened her wicket gate. She went through, then walked up the path, giving a girlish backwards wave. Gosh, she thought, have I lost all my skills?

Seven

The following morning when Kate got downstairs the sun was filling her kitchen, and she thought, Today I'm going to be a villager. She had her breakfast, and because the kitchen was so inviting with the sun streaming in and the view of the garden filling the window, she thought she'd do some baking to keep her there. She felt unexpectedly happy, as if she were bathed in an aura of happiness. Her mind went to Mark Leaver. Was it because of him? But he wasn't a particularly happy person, and there were those peculiar little gaps when he seemed to run out of conversation, as if he was tired of playing a role. Perhaps he still missed his wife. She collected the ingredients she wanted, turned on the oven and set to.

When the telephone rang, Kate answered it absentmindedly, dusting the receiver with flour. She was taken aback to hear John Newton's voice.

'John, I—'

'Please, Kate, there's really no need. When you upped and left I got the message loud and clear.' His voice was icy cool.

'John, I felt I owed it to myself – and you owed it to your wife – to make a clean break. I'm sorry I didn't tell you but '

He cut her short. 'It's probably for the best. Anyway, I'm calling in a professional capacity. How's the next book coming along?'

Relieved at the change of subject, Kate whittled on about

research and distractions before John cut the conversation short with determined professionalism.

'That's good to hear. I look forward to reading the first draft. Goodbye, Kate.'

And with that he was gone.

Well, Kate thought, that could have gone better – but then again, it could have gone a lot worse. She was surprised to realize that she felt nothing but relief that their first encounter was over . . .

Half an hour later, Kate looked at the sponge cake in all its glory, which she had liberally spread with raspberry jam, then powdered with castor sugar on the top. It was inviting, begging to be eaten with its yellow fluffiness, its rich brown casing and its snowy top. She decided to take it to Mrs Paxton. She no doubt had more visitors than Kate. She put it on a pretty plate with a rose border and carried it carefully to Ruth Paxton's door. In a moment she opened it.

'Well, well, what a pleasant surprise!' she said. 'Do come in.'

'I won't. I've been baking this morning, and I thought you'd like a sample.' She proffered the plate with the sponge cake on it.

'Oh, how thoughtful of you! But you must come in. Belle's here. Her mother dropped her in as she's visiting in the village.'

Protesting, Kate was led into the kitchen where Belle was at the sink, apparently washing up. 'Look what Kate has brought us, Belle,' Ruth Paxton said. The girl swivelled round, and while Kate's eyes were on her, there seemed to be a pause as if the world had stopped. Her face changed, became blank, then contorted horribly, and she seemed to crumple before Kate's terrified eyes, and then she was lying on the floor. Kate, hardly believing what she was witnessing but realizing she should be doing something, dumped the cake on a nearby counter, and looked around for Ruth, then she saw she was on the floor beside Belle. She knelt beside her, hearing her heart beating, slow, steady beats of fear. 'Is there anything I can do?' she whispered. She looked at the girl, who was writhing on the floor, her arms and legs flailing, her face contorted, her eyes turned up.

'No, it will soon pass. Would you bring me a cushion from the lounge for her head, please?'

Kate ran into the hall and across it, into the room where she grabbed a cushion from the sofa. Pull yourself together, she told herself. She had never seen anyone having a fit before. She ran back and helped Ruth slip the cushion under Belle's head. She was scarcely recognizable as the laughing girl Kate knew. 'How long does it last?' she whispered.

'A few minutes at the most. You've never seen a grand mal seizure before?' Kate shook her head. 'It's more frightening for the onlooker. See, her limbs are getting quieter already. Belle, Belle!' She bent over her. Kate saw the girl's eyes were still turned up. 'Ruthie's here.' Belle slowly opened her eyes, stared around her and then at Ruth and began struggling to get up, with Ruth helping her.

Belle looked around again, her eyes alighting on Kate. 'Who's that?' she said, pointing at her.

'I'm Kate, from next door.' And because she felt she had to explain her presence, 'I've brought a cake for your morning coffee.'

Belle looked at Ruth. 'Did I do it again?'

'Well, why else would you be lying on the floor? Come on, we're going to help you up to sit on a chair.'

'I was doing your dishes.'

'Well, they can wait. Oops-a-daisy!' Kate helped Ruth to get the girl on to a chair.

'Shall I go?' she asked.

'Not at all. It's business as usual. Stay and have a coffee with us and a piece of your own cake.'

'Well . . .' Kate looked at the girl who now was the Belle she knew. 'Would you like me to do that, Belle? Wouldn't you like to . . .'

'No, she wouldn't like to rest,' Ruth Paxton said. 'She's going to have coffee and cake with us, then she'll finish washing up for me. Won't you, Belle?'

'Yes. Mummy will soon be whisking me away.'

Kate got the feeling that she was more affected by the incident than Belle was. The girl praised the cake, but had orange juice instead of coffee. As soon as she decently could, Kate went back to her own house. At the door, Ruth Paxton said, 'Don't worry. She'll be all right. She won't remember a thing.'

'No, I shan't worry. It's the first fit I've seen,' she said apologetically, 'but of course, I realize Belle won't remember anything. I see there's nothing one can do.'

'Nothing. I hope it won't stop you dropping in – with or without the odd cake.' She smiled at Kate, and closed the door.

When she was in her own house, Kate sat down. Her legs were trembling. Of course, she mustn't make heavy weather of it, and it was a good thing she had witnessed Belle having a fit, she told herself. She would be prepared for the next time. She was sitting beside the telephone, and on an impulse she dialled Jan's number. 'Hello, Jan,' she said, 'how are you?' She wanted to hear a reassuring voice. 'I'm thinking of coming up to town some day next week. Would you like to meet me for lunch?'

'Yes, I would. Are you yearning for the bright lights already?'

'No, it's fine here.' She had a disinclination to talk about Belle, or indeed Mark Leaver. She had the feeling that she was communicating from a different country.

They fixed on Wednesday for the following week, and then she hung up, saying she had to get on. She still felt peculiar, but hadn't Jan sounded restrained, not her usual bubbling voice? I'm imagining things, she told herself. She would go upstairs to her study and mull over her book. She remembered that she had intended to put her father's mahogany clock upstairs. She had taken it from her mother's house when she died – neither Roy or Margaret had wanted it – and she lifted it from its resting place on the mantelpiece of her sitting room. It had never been right there, being of mahogany and waisted in a French design – too dainty, and at odds with the stout oak beams of the ceiling. She carried it carefully upstairs and placed it on the mantelpiece of the study. It wasn't often one had fireplaces in bedrooms. Perhaps it would inspire her. She had planned to make a bright little fire in the fireplace for winter when she was working here. She read the brass inscription on the front of the clock: 'Presented to Robert W. Armitage by a few friends on the occasion of his marriage, on 26th June, 1946'. Who were the few friends? War comrades?

She sat down at her computer, thinking that her father had probably been convivial, hence the inscription on the clock. Had her mother been responsible for choking off the 'few friends'? She didn't remember jovial men, possibly with wives, visiting them. In fact, she didn't remember anyone visiting them. Her mind whirled. This was not a good day for writing, she decided. Perhaps the episode with Belle had upset her.

On the day arranged, Kate went up to London to meet Jan. She didn't take the car, as parking would be too difficult. When she had lived in Islington there had been residents' parking in the square, but it was impossible now.

They met in their favourite restaurant, where Kate got a warm welcome from Mike, the proprietor. 'So you're living in the sticks, now? How does that suit you?'

'It's different,' she said.

When they had ordered, Jan said, 'Is it so different?'

'Yes. One becomes embroiled.' She told her of the episode

with Belle. 'I don't remember in London knowing what was going on around me. Of course there was the office, and the tittle-tattle there. But one could ignore it. Do you miss it?'

'No, but then I had the girls and their lives and helping with their babies when they arrived, and so on. That was why I felt so lonely when that was all over, and was glad to make Nick part of my life. I needed someone. You never seemed to need that. I suppose it's one's upbringing that influences how one lives later. And then marriage and having a family. I missed Joe.'

'Yes, I craved my own life. I thought that was all I wanted. But I knew loneliness, too late.'

'I think I'm going to feel it soon,' Jan said. Kate looked at her. When she had met Jan she had thought she looked pale. Now she noticed the dark shadows under her eyes. 'Why not come and spend some time with me? The country air would do you good.'

'No, I couldn't do that. Things aren't going so well with Nick. I want to be here. It may only be temporary.'

'Is there something bothering you?'

'I hope not. But he goes out without me. It's not someone else, I hope. He's got in with a different crowd, I know. He's cagey. I don't know if there is someone, or if he's getting tired of me. Perhaps I'm not so . . . sprightly as I used to be. Perhaps he's found someone else.'

'Why don't you ask him?'

'I'm afraid. There might be.'

'Well, my suggestion is perfect, then. If you came to me for a while, he would see that you didn't rely on him.' Kate touched Jan's hand. 'Perhaps you'll have to learn not to rely on him.'

'When I was working it didn't seem to matter. Now it does.' Her eyes were full of tears.

'They're not worth it. I tell you what, let's take the Tube to Kew. I always found that beneficial.'

'I haven't your liking for green spaces. I'm a townee.'

'Well, let's go anyway. We'll sit in the sun and have tea outside, and watch the world go by.'

'OK.'

Her beauty is fading, Kate thought, looking at her. She needs a man around to make her bloom.

They passed the afternoon very amicably, even managed to laugh at old jokes, but when Kate was speeding back on the train, she felt sad for Jan. She collected her car at Leeston station where she had parked it, and felt glad. There were cars at the Hare and Hounds, and she remembered the names of the owners, Cyril and Judy Grantham. When she was unlocking her door, she saw the roses round it needed pruning. She had a sense of coming home.

Eight

The apple tree was laden with fruit – Bramleys, Mark Leaver had told her. She would pick a few and make some apple tarts, put some in the freezer. She was washing up after breakfast and looking out at the garden, pleased with the difference Mark Leaver had made in it. The beds of flowers were blooming, and the little waterfall was doing what it was supposed to do, tumbling over the stones and falling into the pool with a pleasant splash. She might buy a single water lily, and plant it – there wasn't room for more. Meantime there was an October sun shining, and everything looked copper coloured. She would make some coffee and take it out to her seat, also some seed for the birds. Miss Thom must have been a bird lover. There was a bird table placed near the window, and hooks for titbits. She would have to save any fat from cooking, bacon rinds and such, and put them in a net bag and hang it up.

Oh, you're so busy! she said to herself, amused at what could fill her mind compared with her work at the office – possibly reading Lily Rose's slush, and estimating if it would hit the jackpot again. The telephone rang and she went to answer it, hoping it wasn't John Newton. She heard Mark Leaver's voice.

'Are you busy? I hope I haven't interrupted anything.'

'Except for feeding the birds, then I was going to sit in the shade of the old apple tree and admire what you've done.'

'I'm glad you're pleased. I've got a favour to ask of you.

I've got two tickets for a concert in the Wigmore Hall on Saturday. Would you like to come with me – that is, if you like Mozart?'

'I'm just beginning to recognize his works from the other composers. I'm a complete ignoramus when it comes to music. But I'm prepared to go with you and join in the applause when I should.'

'Would it be a complete bore to you? Perhaps I could tempt you with an early dinner beforehand?'

'I don't need to be tempted, but that would be nice.'

'Good. I'll call for you at five thirty. Would that suit? I know where to park.'

'That would suit me very well. And thank you for the invitation.' She waited for him to say something, and after an appreciable pause she heard him say, 'Good!' and hang up. She went on with what she was doing, thinking of him, puzzling about him. It was a long time since she had had an invitation from a man. John Newton had absorbed her free time.

She was ready for him on Saturday when he called. 'This is nice,' she said as he helped her into the car. 'Do you know, I'm ashamed to say that although I lived in London for so long, I've never been in the Wigmore Hall.'

'I gather you're not an afficionado, then?'

'Regrettably, no. I suppose it all depends on one's upbringing.'

'Perhaps. Ours was quite a musical family. My mother was a pianist, and she encouraged my sister and myself to play an instrument, mine was the flute. We used to have quite good times playing together, and then I discovered the keyboard, and did quite well with that, much to her disapproval.'

'No, we had nothing like that. Although my mother once said to me that my father went to concerts when he could, but she had refused to go with him, especially to opera. "Who wants to hear fat women screeching?" she once said to me. He died when I was very young, so perhaps I should have been influenced by him.'

'Perhaps her talents lay in other directions?'

Kate thought. Which directions? Her mother's talents had lain in making dresses for Kate. Undiscovered creativity? It had never occurred to her before, but she had never seen her mother reading, except a newspaper. Her mother's father had been an architect, and his wife had been incarcerated in some kind of home for many years. There might well be some kind of artistic background there. 'I have vague memories of my father singing, but we certainly weren't encouraged in that direction, although Glasgow was a good centre, for operatic societies,' she said.

A memory came back to Kate of a friend of her father's who continued to visit them after he had died. Her mother had been quite ungracious to Miss Robinson – 'Here's that old biddy again,' she would say when she saw her coming up the garden path. Miss Robinson's visits, probably motivated out of kindness, had slowly dwindled and stopped.

Dragging herself out of her reverie, she turned to Mark and said, 'A friend of my father's, Miss Robinson, I remember once asked me to sell programmes at a production of "Cav and Pag", as she called it. She was a member of an amateur operatic group. I remember some of the songs to this day. During the performance I was told to sit in a side seat, ready to spring up with my programmes at the interval.'

'Well, that, at least, was an introduction,' Mark said. 'Do you remember Pagliacci's aria?'

'Yes.' She remembered the wrench she'd felt, in her heart, listening to the lead singer. 'To this day.' To her surprise, Mark burst into the aria, '*I Pagliacci . . .*' The very one she remembered.

When he had finished, he said, 'Was it that one? It's broken many hearts, as well as his own.'

'That's it. Heart-rending to a young girl. You've a good voice,' she said.

'Thank you.' He laughed.

Their conversation seemed to break the ice, and she suddenly found she could talk to him easily. Gone were the awkward pauses. She told him about visiting the Tate while living in London. Usually she had gone alone. She had followed lecturers around the National Gallery, and the Tate, listening avidly, and had tried to back it up with reading, but she had never known anyone with whom she could share her interest. John had monopolized most of her free time – or according to Jan, Kate had allowed this to happen.

I think I'll concentrate on art now that I have more time, she thought. There's a whole world there waiting to be discovered. Mark Leaver seemed to stimulate her, to open avenues down which she now had time to go. Life seemed suddenly to open out to her; there were wonderful things to discover, countries to visit. And there was her writing. Recently she had been experiencing what she thought might be called 'writer's block'. She must make time for the computer, every day.

When they were driving home after the concert, where Kate had decided she was tone deaf, Mark said, 'Did you enjoy yourself?'

'I recognized some of the melodies, strange to say. Yes, thank you, I've enjoyed my evening, and the dinner, and your company.'

He put a hand over hers. 'I'm glad, Kate. We'll do it again. I'm afraid I'm out of practise, but since Sheila died . . .'

When they reached Leeston, he took the road that led round the Green and down Vicarage Lane, instead of the more direct route to her cottage.

'Isn't this . . .?' she said looking out of the window, and discovering she was on the far side of the Green.

'Yes, I've taken the long way home. Trying to extend our

evening together,' he said. 'I thought I might stop here and say goodnight, instead of compromising you by stopping at your gate. You know what it's like in villages.'

'Well, why not compromise me further and come in for a drink?' she said. She was amused at herself. He would take the remark as a direct invitation to further intimacy, instead of which it had been a throwaway remark on her part.

'Thank you,' he said, 'perhaps I shall.'

The road was very dark with no lighting except for the car's headlights. They swept over hedges, fields and trees, and lit up the vicarage and the road ahead. She thought there were two people walking some distance away, but couldn't be sure. 'Do you think that's a couple ahead?' she asked him. She looked at her watch. 'Twelve o'clock,' she said, 'someone's out late.'

He passed the couple. Kate swivelled round in her seat, and tried to pierce the darkness with her eyes. Horror suddenly filled her. They looked like Belle Dexter and Garry Fox, but that was ridiculous! She waited till her heart slowed down and then turned to Mark. 'Do you know,' she said, steadying her voice, 'for a minute, I could have sworn that was Belle Dexter and Garry Fox.'

He didn't reply for an instant. 'Surely not! But the man did seem familiar . . . I thought of Garry Fox. He has a reputation in the village. But I don't know who the woman might have been. It couldn't have been Belle Dexter. She's a child. She would be in bed by now.' They were passing the village pond now. He slowed down at the junction of the roads, peering both ways. He's forgotten he was going to stop to say goodnight, Kate thought. 'She had a scarf over her head,' he said.

'You're right. Belle couldn't be out with Garry Fox at this time. She's safely in bed.' Still, she thought, the girl's fifteen. Ruth Paxton's remark came into her head: she's sexually aware.

'Well, we can't turn back and question him,' he said. 'He's entitled to have a tryst with a young lady of the village, if he wants.'

'Yes, I suppose so.' But we could have turned back, she thought, knowing that would be silly.

She was so perturbed that when he pulled up at her gate and looked expectantly at her, she quite forgot about her earlier invitation. 'Thank you so much, Mark,' she said, 'it's been a lovely evening.' She leaned towards him and kissed his cheek. 'Goodnight.' She got out of the car, ran up the path, unlocked the door and went straight to the kitchen. She'd make herself some coffee.

What was I thinking about, she thought, snubbing him like that? She carried her cup of coffee into the sitting room. It was cold and unwelcoming, and she put on all the lights and sat down. 'Get a grip' used to be the saying in the office. You saw the vicarage which made you think of Belle probably, then you saw two people walking. Mark identified Garry Fox, and he must know Belle too, but he didn't suggest that it could have been her. She had a scarf over her head, he said. And whoever it was had been wearing a dark coat. Belle is slim, she reminded herself, like hundreds of young girls. You've never studied her, how she might look from behind. What an outrageous idea of yours to assume that she was the girl walking beside Garry Fox! You had nothing to go on except that her head came up to his shoulder. As far as she remembered Garry Fox was a medium tall young man, and Belle seemed smaller.

She drank her coffee. It would be ridiculous to telephone the vicarage on such an assumption. But would she regret it if she didn't? She didn't want to give the Dexters the impression that she was an excitable woman. Leave it, she told herself. Concentrate on your rudeness to Mark Leaver. He's obviously shy or he would have reminded you of your earlier remark about coming into the house. But it was a silly remark and she didn't really want to start something.

She would telephone him tomorrow and apologize, make light of it. After all, he had said he intended to stop in Vicarage Lane and he hadn't done it. She went to bed, thoroughly disturbed. It had been a pleasant evening, but whether she would have thought more about Mark Leaver if it hadn't been for seeing Garry Fox with a young woman whom she had *thought* might have been Belle Dexter, she couldn't decide. She tossed and turned for a long time before she slept.

The next morning, before she got downstairs, Mark telephoned her. 'Kate,' he said, 'I'm phoning to apologize. When you didn't ask me in last night, I thought you'd changed your mind. I wish I were more forceful.'

'Rubbish,' she said, 'I don't like forceful men. But you did say you were going to stop in Vicarage Lane, and I imagined you'd thought better of it. I was perturbed at seeing that couple, and wanted to be alone.'

'I quite understand, but I'm sure you were wrong. Belle would never be out with Garry at that time. As I said, he has a reputation in the village. To make amends, would you have a drink at the Hare and Hounds with me on Saturday evening?'

'That would be nice. And why not come back with me for supper?'

'Are you sure?'

'Sure. I'm good at whipping up late-night suppers.' She remembered John arriving late at her flat and saying he hadn't eaten, and they would decide to have a snack after . . . I don't miss him, she thought.

Mark and I could have eaten at the pub, she suddenly thought, when she was downstairs preparing her breakfast. Well, why didn't you say so? she thought. And then, Why do you keep issuing invitations to this man and then regret them?

* * *

They were welcomed at the bar by Cyril Grantham. 'Hello, there,' he said to Kate. 'You want to watch this man,' he put a hand on Mark's shoulder. 'He's known in the village as a ladykiller.'

'Pay no attention to him, Kate,' Mark said. 'Let's find a table.' He put an arm round her, and led her to a table at the back of the room. Cyril Grantham was behind them.

'We haven't been officially introduced,' he said, pulling out chairs for them. 'Mark's got ahead of me.'

'Kate Armitage,' Mark said. 'And this is Cyril Grantham. Will that do?'

'You came with a friend a few weeks ago,' Grantham said to Kate. 'How are you settling down?'

'Very well.' She smiled at him. She was more familiar with Grantham's type than Mark Leaver. She couldn't quite fathom him. There's no oomph, she thought.

'What can I get you, then?' he said looking from Mark to her.

'Kate?'

'A glass of white wine, dry.'

'I know Madame's predilection,' Cyril Grantham said. 'It's Sauvignon Blanc. We keep a nice one here.'

'Good for you,' Kate said.

'Is he treating you to one of our famous dinners?'

'Not tonight, Cyril,' Mark said.

'Right, I know Mark's choice. Beer, isn't it?'

Mark nodded. 'Your special, thanks.'

When he had gone, Mark said to Kate, 'You have to watch old Cyril. He never seems to know when to go.' She didn't reply and he went on, 'Judy owns the pub. She inherited it from her father. Cyril's fallen on his feet.'

He looked enquiringly at her. 'Are you sure you want me to come back for supper?' he said. He looked uneasy.

'Of course.'

They talked, but not in the easy way they had when they had gone to London. Once when there was a pause, and

Kate was looking at the bar from their table, she said, 'I've never met Cyril's wife.' She was officiating there, smilingly at ease with the people around.

'I'll introduce you on the way out,' he said.

'I'm ready now. Shall we go, then?'

'OK.' He drained his glass and stood up. So did Kate. They stopped at the bar, and Mark caught the woman's eye. She came over to them, smiling. 'Well, Mark, nice to see you.'

'Kate would like to meet you, Judy. She's recently come to live in the village. Kate Armitage.'

'Oh, yes. I think Cyril mentioned you.' She held out her hand across the bar. Her eyes were steady, with a hint of laughter in them. She's a person I could tell about that couple we saw, Kate thought.

'Have you settled down?'

'Yes. I like it. So handy for London.'

'Yes, that's its advantage. Excuse me, some thirsty people here.' A group of men were waiting with empty glasses. 'See you around, then. The hub of the village is the WI. Has Barbara Dexter winkled you in there?'

'Not yet. I thought I might volunteer for the crèche.'

'They'll be glad to have you, I'm sure. I'll say goodbye, then.' She left them, and they heard her cheerful voice speaking to the new arrivals. 'Good evening. What can I get you?'

'I like her,' Kate said as they went out to the car. The front of the pub was lit up, and backed by trees. She thought it was what a country pub should look like. There was a burst of laughter, probably from the men at the bar. But it's no different from any place in London, except for the trees and the window boxes of flowers, she thought. You've seen it on calendars often. She felt apprehensive as she sat beside Mark, driving towards her house. She would rather have remained at the pub.

'Shall we eat in the kitchen?' she said, as she led him into the hall.

'Suits me. I often do that. Sheila liked it. We have a big kitchen. It's one of the older houses, but I haven't en suite bathrooms like the new houses where Lorna and Roger Crook are.'

'They're a delightful couple. And that little boy . . .'

'She wants to get back to work, she's confided to me. She supplies shops in London and she's fearful that she'll lose their custom.'

'Couldn't she work at home and keep an eye on Seb?'

'One would think so, but I think she's single-minded.'

'Well, she'll have to work it out for herself. I imagine he's a planned baby. I should say she's not in the first flush of youth – her thirties, perhaps.'

'She's lucky to have him. We couldn't have any. Sheila was so disappointed.'

I don't want to know, Kate thought, changing the subject. 'Do you like kedgeree?' She took out a salad of avacados and lettuce from the refrigerator. 'Shall we have a drink while we're waiting for it to heat?'

'That would be nice.' She had reached into the fridge again and taken out a bottle of Sauvignon Blanc. He took the bottle from her, looked at the label and said, 'Good choice.' Then, 'corkscrew?' He raised his eyebrows. Make yourself at home, she thought. Why was she so bitchy about him?

They chatted together during the meal, mostly about Sheila, his wife. She grew tired pretending interest, and said, 'Why don't we watch the news? I never feel I've ended the day properly if I miss it.'

'Right.' He followed her and settled himself down on the sofa beside her, putting his arm along her shoulders. 'Lovely meal, Kate,' he said turning to her. He breathed fish on her. She probably did the same on him. Why was it that the smell of fish lingered so long? His hand slipped down and fondled her breast. 'Please, Mark,' she said.

'Not in the mood?' he said

'I'm too old to go in for canoodling on a couch.' She attempted a laugh. Her mind went back to Gavin, and how they had both felt eager at the same time, and then John, which had been premeditated, a prearranged thing each time; no doubt about what he was there for. I've missed out, she thought. I've made a terrible mess of my life. Mark Leaver probably didn't know the moves, because of his marriage. He had lost the knack; she had never known it.

'I'm not very good at it either,' he said. 'Am I supposed to overpower you, or get you so drunk that you're a willing victim?'

'I think we should just watch the news,' she said, 'and not jump the gun.'

'I think you're right. I could grow very fond of you, Kate, and it seems so right that you should arrive here just when I was getting over Sheila.'

'Supposing we start by being friends?'

'You're right. Well, I'll finish my coffee.'

'I think that's best.'

When he had gone she thought, Well, that was a failure. You're happy in your cottage, Kate, and with your writing. Let things evolve. She went upstairs and sat in front of her computer, turned back to the last chapter she had written. She found her block had gone. She typed until two in the morning, happy.

George had driven into the village, intent on buying some buckets from Mackie's, the hardware shop. 'Not yellow plastic,' Isobel had said. 'They're an eyesore lying about the yard.' He was just paying Mr Mackie, and joking about the amount of plastic he was selling, when he heard Peter McCosh's voice. He was standing beside him. 'George is quite right, Mackie. Don't let plastic go to your head.'

George turned. 'Hello, Peter. What are you doing here? Neglecting your patients?'

They chatted for a few moments, ribbing Mackie, then arranged to meet in the Anvil for a drink. They had been schoolboys together and Isobel was friendly with Mollie, Peter's wife. He was the local doctor.

'Well, George, long time no see.' Peter sat down beside him in a corner of the pub a few minutes later. 'As a matter of fact I wanted a word with you . . . Hi, Tom!' – this to one of his patients, whom George knew. Peter, when he succeeded his father, had made a point of being seen at the Anvil. He believed his patients approved, especially the young men of the village.

'What did you want to see me about?' George raised his glass.

'It's very personal. But this is as good a place as any.' He leaned forward, lowering his voice. 'Rumour has it that you're seeing a lot of Anne Kay.'

'What the devil . . .!' George spluttered.

'*Now, don't get rattled. I've wanted to fill you in about her family. It's my duty, as a friend and a doctor.*'

'*Go on.*' *George felt a sense of dread.*

'*Both Mrs Collins, the housekeeper, and Anne have been my patients. Indeed, Mrs Collins has confided in me . . .*' *He looked quizzically at George.* '*People think Anne isn't a good match for you . . .*' *George looked down at his glass. His heart was racing. Hadn't he had doubts about Anne, the way she looked at him, her secrecy, her comments about people in the village?*

'*The point is, George,*' *Peter went on,* '*Mrs Collins has told me that Mary Kay, Anne's mother, comes from a very dubious family background. She knew them when they arrived in Glasgow, there were rumours about them, that they moved frequently to avoid the debts they had collected. But never mind that. Mary Kay made a good marriage, and had a child, Anne. The doctor in Glasgow was worried when she didn't recover from postnatal depression, and sent her to see a psychiatrist. Her condition didn't improve, and she got into a state where she refused to speak. Psychiatry was not very advanced in those days, and eventually her husband was advised to have her incarcerated for the sake of his daughter and himself. He admitted that she had always had a difficult temperament, almost from the first day of his marriage.*'

'*Would you like another?*' *George pointed at Peter's glass. I'm hearing something that affects me, he thought. He was shaken.*

'*No, thank you. Not in front of my patients. And I advise you not to take that route. I can see you're affected by what I've told you.*'

'*I must admit I am.*' *George wiped his forehead.* '*I know Anne is deeply disappointed that I didn't propose marriage, but at times I felt she was . . . strange. Unfortunately she didn't seem to have much of a rapport with Mrs Collins, but she found a friend in Isobel. Mixed with my love of Anne I think both Isobel and I felt sorry for her.'*

Peter nodded. *'Mrs Collins was a friend and a widow, and when Bruce Kay agreed to Mary being incarcerated in a home outside Glasgow, Mrs Collins offered to help him out in the household with Anne. She told me that Anne was "difficult" as a child, and she hadn't thought it a good idea for her to be taken to see her mother. When she grew up she suffered from temper tantrums, and Mrs Collins could feel quite afraid of her on occasion. She would have liked to move out, but Bruce Kay, Anne's father, begged her to stay on as housekeeper. He spent a lot of time in Glasgow, from the time he took over his father's house here. Indeed, Mrs Collins thought he had a woman friend there – and who could blame him?'*

'So are people in the village talking about me?' Bitterness rose in George's throat. He had always wanted to marry, to raise a family, to carry on the name of Armitage. To be like his father. He looked at Peter.

'Don't take this so badly, George. I thought it only fair to tell you about Anne's background, because I have a great regard for you.'

'Did these doctors ever put a name to the condition?'

'I don't know. In my experience there are a lot of people going about who are fragile, can't cope, have never been able to deal with life, though are generally intelligent.' He looked at his watch. 'The afternoon surgery will be waiting for me. I talked this over with Mollie, and she thought I should tell you. I see now I've passed on the load to you. But you and I have always been good pals. Forgive me if I've done the wrong thing.' He got up and put his hand on George's shoulder as he moved away.

'Well, George,' it was Simmons, the contractor. 'Is the doctor leading you into bad habits?'

George got up. 'Far from it. We ran into each other. Any objections?' He had never liked the man.

'No. Nothing at all. I was just going to ask you if you would have a pint with me.'

'Sorry, I'm late already. Isobel will be fuming.' He strode out of the pub. He imagined that heads were together talking about him.

Nine

The following morning Kate answered her door to Barbara Dexter. 'Well, this is a nice surprise,' she said. 'Come in and have a cup of coffee.'

'I can't refuse, because I have a favour to ask you.' She wore her usual charming smile.

'Come in.' Is it about Belle? Kate thought. And once they were sitting having their coffee, she asked, 'How's Belle?'

'Oh, she's fine, but we're getting a little impatient with the school she's supposed to be going to. We haven't heard from them yet. She's restless, and I'm afraid Ralph is a little impatient with her. You know, Daddy's girl! He forgets she's fifteen now, and she objects to being treated as a child.'

Kate could imagine the situation. He was disappointed that his daughter was flawed, couldn't accept it. But he's a vicar, she thought. And then, Does he go to extremes and try to regulate her behaviour, and as a result she rebels and slips out to meet Garry Fox?

To stop her train of thought, she said, 'Fire away. You said you had a favour to ask of me?'

'Oh, yes, it's about the WI. Mabel Rossiter, who is our programmes secretary, has to go to New Zealand to visit her married daughter. She's arranged for an American woman living in London to come and talk to us about life over there, and Mabel had promised to meet her at the station. The Embassy are very particular. The women do these talks for free, but they must have first-class travel and be shepherded from the station and back again. I never thought of American women as not being able to take care of themselves, but there it is. They don't charge for their talk, and we were pleased to accept their offer.'

'So you want me to meet this woman and take charge of her?'

'Yes, that's it. Of course, you will be our guest too. Maybe you'll like it so much that you'll want to join the WI.' She smiled at Kate.

'Maybe. I did say to someone the other day that I might volunteer to look after the crèche.'

'Really? Well, you'd be very welcome to come on our rota. You're a real brick, Kate. Shall I call for you for the next meeting, which is October the 24th, and you can get all the particulars about meeting the American lady from Mabel?'

'All right. What time?'

'About two o'clock. Mabel will be there early. The meeting starts at two thirty. Perhaps you'll stay on for it?'

'Perhaps.' Kate laughed. 'I never thought of myself at the WI.'

'It's not all about how to make raspberry jam, I can assure you. Well, I'm going to be rude, Kate, and take myself off. I have to look in and see the twins. Jane Driver, who helps me at the vicarage, tells me that they have been seen wandering about the Nettlefields.'

'The Nettlefields?'

'It's what we call the land at the top of Nettlebed Lane. It was all Colonel Blue's garden at one time, but then he gave an acre of it to the council and built a wall dividing it from his garden. The council didn't use all of the acre for their houses, and there is a spare piece of unused land. The wall dividing it from the Blues' garden has deteriorated over the years. There has been a dispute for ages about who should repair this wall, but you know what councils are like. It's their responsibility, one would think, but Edna has had some tussles with them.'

'You can't expect two old ladies to bother themselves about that.'

'Not when they're nearing eighty.' She looked at Kate. 'Why don't you come with me and be introduced? They'll be delighted. They treat any newcomers as serfs. It's quite amusing.'

'I'm fascinated. You're sure they won't mind?'

'Oh, no. They have a dull life. It will be nice for them.'

'All right. Let me get my coat.'

She sat beside Barbara, being driven to Nettlebed Lane. Barbara Dexter was a terrible driver, or perhaps just enthusiastic. She constantly blew her horn at any passers-by, bending over the wheel and waving enthusiastically, or indicated by a wave anything of interest to Kate – a favourite tree, or where her friend, Dolly, had lived before she went to Italy – or braked precipitately to avoid a dog that might have strayed from the council estate. Opposite the houses, she took a right turn down a lane, at the end of which there was a gate, which was shut. 'Bother,' she said. 'I'll have to get out.'

'Let me,' Kate said, scrambling out of the car. She released the latch of a huge rusty gate. Ahead of her she could see a sizeable stone house with mullioned windows. It looked forbidding because of the overgrown bushes and the lack of flowerbeds. What had been lawns were uncut and straggly. Couldn't they pay for a gardener? she wondered.

Barbara said, when Kate had got back in the car, 'They've never forgiven Sheila Leaver for dying. She had started on redesigning their garden, and had roped in Garry Fox to help her. I don't think he's turned up since.'

Kate glanced at Barbara when she mentioned Garry Fox, but it didn't seem to be anything more than a casual remark. The image of Garry and the young woman Kate still suspected might have been Belle rose unbidden before her eyes. She shook her head.

Barbara rang the bell when they had climbed the stone

steps to the house, and in a short time a small, mouse-faced woman opened the door. She looked to Kate as if she had strayed from Beatrix Potter's books. She brightened when she saw Barbara.

'Hello Edna,' Barbara said. 'I've brought a newcomer to see you.'

The woman swept a penetrating glance over Kate. Her black eyes were shrewd. 'Oh, yes, come in, please. Eva will be pleased to see you.' She led the way into a huge sitting room where the other twin, presumably, was sitting. To her surprise, Kate saw that this one was a bigger edition altogether, a huge woman with the same features as her sister, but softer altogether, and her eyes were like those of a trusty dog. 'Hello, Barbara,' she said, getting up and bending forward to kiss her on the cheek, 'How nice to see you. It's been a long time.'

'Yes, I'm sorry, but you've had a visit from Belle, haven't you?'

'Yes,' she looked doubtfully at her sister. 'Has Belle called lately, Edna?'

'Of course she has. Don't you remember?' Her tone was sharp, though she didn't seem any more convinced than her sister.

'Kate Armitage has come to live in the village.' Barbara looked at Kate. 'I thought you'd like to meet her.'

'Oh, that's nice,' Eva said. 'We're always pleased to meet newcomers, aren't we, Edna? When Father was here we used to—'

'Don't start on your reminiscences,' Edna said sharply. 'Of course we are. Is it mistress or miss?' She held out her hand to Kate.

'I'm unmarried. But please call me Kate.'

'Don't worry,' she said. 'We don't mind.'

'We used to worry about not being married,' Eva said. 'We talked about it, didn't we Edna, wondered what it would be like.'

'I don't remember that,' her sister said, quailing the bigger woman with a look.

'Yes, we did,' Eva said. 'Don't you remember you told me . . .'

Edna gave Kate and Barbara a meaningful look, as if to apologize for her sister. 'She does ramble on.' She turned to her sister. 'Suppose you go and make some tea for our visitors, Eva?'

'Oh, yes, that would be a good idea. I'll do that right away. Is it too early for sherry, Edna?'

'Of course it is. Please sit down, Miss Armitage, and you too, Barbara.'

Barbara rushed into speech. 'It's much too early for tea, Edna. In any case, I shall have to be back for Ralph's.'

'Well, supposing we have a walk round the garden? Eva and I generally do that after lunch. Don't bother with tea, Eva. You can come along with us.'

The other twin simpered, and said to Barbara and Kate, 'I'd much rather come along with you anyway. I can show you my garden.'

They all trooped out with Kate wondering where the garden was. Walking down an overgrown drive, Barbara said, 'Hasn't Garry Fox come back to help you? Sheila had him all organized.'

'No, he hasn't – not to tend the garden, at least, though we've seen him in the Nettlefields.' The smaller twin looked disdainful.

'He asked Edna for a fearful amount of money,' her sister said.

'Sheila hadn't mentioned money,' the smaller sister said. 'But we weren't going to be taken in by that man, oh, dear no!'

'Oh, dear no!' her sister chorused.

Kate noticed the old stone wall which bordered the whole of the garden, and that in some places it had collapsed, showing the nettle-covered ground on the other side. So did

Barbara, evidently. 'Your wall is needing attention, I'm afraid. Nothing's been done about it, then?'

'No. They asked us to come to a meeting, but of course, I refused.'

'She was quite right,' Eva said. 'It's round here.' They had reached a path going off at a tangent. 'My garden.'

Her sister gave Barbara and Kate a disparaging glance. 'Yes,' she said, 'we must see Eva's garden.'

Certainly it was October, Kate thought, but the garden, if it ever had been good, was a sorry sight. Everything was withered, although there were a few brilliantly-coloured dahlias.

'My dahlias have done well this year,' Eva said.

'They're lovely,' Kate said enthusiastically. 'But, of course, it's not a good time for gardens. There's always gorse, of course. That brilliant yellow.' What a tyro I am, she thought. Gorse grew wild on the hills around Glasgow, not in gardens.

'Oh, yes. I wish I had thought of that. Gorse time is kissing time, they used to say.' She giggled and her sister gave her a look.

'Kate has just had her garden revamped,' Barbara said. 'Miss Thom's old house.'

'Mary Thom,' Edna said, 'another one who wasn't married.'

Kate felt uneasy. The smaller twin was really objectionable, especially to her bigger sister, who, despite her size, was a pathetic creature, she thought. Had Barbara noticed it?

'Have you got spring bulbs in?' she asked Eva. 'I could give you some. I've heaps of daffodils ready to go in, if you'd like them.'

'Oh, that would be lovely!' Eva clapped her hands delightedly.

'It was Mark Leaver who planned my garden for me,' Kate said.

'Yes, Sheila had ideas for mine too, and then she died. She was very kind.'

'He could have come and helped you,' her sister said.

Eva laughed. 'Edna always wants everything for nothing.' Kate saw her sister's face darken. 'Well, that's enough talk about gardens,' she said. 'Shall we go back to the house?'

'We'd love to,' Barbara said, 'but I told you about Ralph and his tea. He depends on me making it.'

'What's wrong with Belle?' Edna said. 'She's a big girl now.'

'But not a substitute for me, I'm afraid.'

'We enjoy her dropping in to see us,' Eva said, 'don't we, Edna?'

'Yes, we're fond of Belle. She's one of our regular visitors. She's a good deputy for you, Barbara, and we do realize you're too busy these days with the WI and everything.' She sighed. 'Those were the days. Can you believe it, I once was president?' She smiled and looked quite animated. 'But the village isn't the same nowadays. Father, of course, held it together. We did try to emulate him, but we have so much to do . . .' Her relief at their imminent departure was evident. She walked towards the car while she was speaking.

'Here we are,' Barbara said, 'so we'll leave you here. It's been so nice to see you both.'

'And very nice to meet your new friend,' Edna smiled at Kate, a winning smile, which made Kate wonder if she had misjudged the woman.

They shook hands, and Kate said to the bigger sister, 'I won't forget about the daffodils. And perhaps you would both like to look in some time?' She was feeling sorry for Eva, but regretted her invitation as soon as she made it.

'Oh, no,' the smaller sister drew herself up. 'We don't visit now, since we gave up the car.'

'Such a pity we're without transport,' Eva simpered.

'It cost too much, don't you remember?' her sister said with a silencing look. Eva looked abashed.

'Well, goodbye,' Kate said. 'It's been a pleasure to meet you both.'

'You're welcome to drop in any time.' The bigger twin put an arm around the shoulder of the smaller one. 'And don't forget to bring the daffodils when you come.' She looked suddenly assertive.

They are a comical pair, Kate thought, as she sat beside Barbara, who was backing the car. She'll never make it through the gates. And then, Is comical the right word to describe the sisters? Or is sinister even better?

She waited until Barbara spoke when they were driving down Nettlebed Lane. 'Well, what did you think of the irrepressible twins?'

'You're used to them, of course . . .'

'Yes, I suppose they are a bit odd. But they're accepted in the village.'

'I felt they were in the wrong bodies.'

Barbara turned to look at her, amused. 'What do you mean?'

'I suppose it's a funny thing to say. But the smaller one seems the bossy one, and her sister seemed to be somewhat under her thumb.'

'I suppose you may be right. But when they were younger, they looked more like twins. Then, I suppose it would be round about the menopause, Eva put on a lot of weight. I often wonder if Edna got at her, you know what I mean.'

'Yes, could be. They seem genuinely fond of Belle.'

'Yes, I was surprised at that. I'm afraid I don't always know what she gets up to. I'm so busy, and Ralph . . .'

'Well, she's doing them a good turn, anyway.'

'Yes, but it's not ideal. You can see why I want her away at school. I'm too busy to know what she gets up to half the time.'

Kate thought about mentioning Garry Fox, but thought better of it.

Barbara dropped Kate at her cottage. 'Don't forget the WI,' she said. 'Next week. I'll pick you up.'

'There's no need, thank you, Barbara. I'll walk along myself.'

'OK. See you.'

When Kate opened her door she heard her telephone ringing. She ran quickly into her lounge and lifted the receiver. She heard Jan's voice.

'Hello, Kate. I'm phoning to tell you that Nick has decamped. So that's that.' Her voice was shaky.

'Oh, no, Jan,' she said. 'Did he explain why?'

'Yes, he's come out with it. He's met someone at this health club he goes to. He gave me the chance to go along with him but I turned it down. I'm not very good on the sports side . . . except in bed.' She laughed.

'Well, I wouldn't know. Is it getting to you?'

'Yes, it is. I have a horrid feeling that that's my romantic life over, that there won't be anyone else.'

'Oh, Jan.' Kate could imagine how she felt. A partner seemed necessary to her well-being. 'Look, why don't you come down here for the weekend and get it off your chest?' There was a pause.

'Would you mind if I accept? I'm due to go to Ros's to dog-sit in a week's time, they're going to Teneriffe, but if I could fill in with you, that would be grand. At the moment I can't face the empty house.'

'Pack up and come right away. I'll be glad to see you.'

'Are you sure? I feel such a wimp.'

'Yes, I'm sure. It would be lovely to see you. We can walk a lot.'

'Now that I've phoned you I feel much better.'

'But you won't tonight. I know you. You can't bear your own company for long. You'll only get depressed.'

'I am. It's a miserable feeling.'

'I'll cheer you up. I'll tell you about the people here, and believe me, some of them are odd.'

'I know you. You'll cope with that. You don't allow yourself to get involved.'

'That's not strictly true. I was involved with John for ten years.'

'But you kept him to one part of your life.'

'You mean, he kept me to one part of *his* life. It was a mutual arrangement. I'm glad I'm out of that.' She thought, I'm not going to talk about John Newton. That was a mistake, we're both well out of it.

That evening at about six o'clock, Kate heard her bell ring. When she opened the door, Mark Leaver was standing there. He was smiling. 'I'm dropping in at the pub for a pint. I'm fed up with plants. Would you like to come along?'

'That would be nice.' She felt pleased that he had thought of her. Her visit to the twins had upset her in a peculiar way, but there was Jan. 'I'll come as I am,' she said. 'Wait till I get my key.'

When they were driving to the pub, she said, 'Barbara Dexter took me to see the Blue twins.'

'Oh, yes. What did you think of them?'

'Edna seems to be the boss.'

'Yes, it's comical. But that has developed over the years, I'm told. There's something nasty about Edna, I find. Sheila used to say that she was puzzled about her. She went up there a fair amount. We only had one car and I used to drive her to their house, so got to know them quite well. I think she's mean. I used to say that to Sheila, but she wouldn't have it. When I said that I was afraid of Edna, she laughed at me. But Sheila always saw the good in everyone.'

She sounds like an exemplary character, Kate thought. And little Edna took advantage of that and accepted the work she did in the garden for free.

They parked at the pub and went in. There was only one table occupied, possibly because it was early, and Cyril and Judy were behind the bar. 'Hi, folks!' Cyril said.

'At least we've time to talk to you,' his wife said. 'How are you, Kate?'

'Fine. I've even got roped in to go to the WI. Barbara Dexter has asked me to stand in for someone while they're in New Zealand.'

'Oh, that's Mabel Rossiter. She's going to New Zealand to see her daughter. She's due to have a baby, and she wants Mummy.'

'Understandable.' Everybody knows everybody's affairs, she thought. I wonder what they say about me?

'She was a sweet girl. Remember Lila Rossiter, Cyril? We had a send-off for her before she went to New Zealand.'

'Yes, not pioneering material, our Lila,' he said. 'A smart London girl. But we could say that about you, couldn't we, Kate?' He looked at her, smiling.

'Scarcely a girl.' He had placed a glass of white wine in front of her. 'On the house. I may forget a name, but never anyone's tipple.'

'Oh, thank you. I must come often. As a matter of fact, I've got a friend coming to stay with me so I daresay I'll be popping in with her.'

'That's nice for you,' Judy said. 'New faces are welcome around here.'

'Why don't you come for tea and meet Jan?' Kate said. 'I'll give you a ring when she arrives this weekend.'

'I'd like that, if this slave-master will let me off.' She looked at her husband.

'Glad to get rid of you,' he said.

'This is typical of the Granthams,' Mark said. 'Go at each other all the time. Don't be taken in.'

'How clever of you to spot it,' Cyril said. 'Yes, you should see us at home. We bill and coo together like a pair of doves.'

'Kate's been visiting the old twins at Nettlebed Lane,' Mark said.

'What did you think of them, Kate?' Judy asked.

'Quite unique. You won't have them dropping in for a pint.'

'That's where you're wrong,' Cyril said. 'Rumour has it that they can knock it back. They have frequent casks delivered from a supplier in Leeston whom I happen to know. He told me they go through the Amontillado.'

'And yet they're mean about other things,' Judy said. 'We're filling up, Cyril. We'll have to stop chatting.'

'I'll give you a ring when Jan comes,' Kate said. She had finished her wine. 'Another?' Mark said.

'No, thank you.'

They soon left, as the Granthams were being kept busy at the bar. On the way back, Mark said, 'Is your guest the one who was having dinner with you a few weeks ago?'

'Yes, Jan Cox. We worked together.'

'A good-looking lady. She reminded me of Sheila.'

'Yes? She appeals to the opposite sex, Jan.' Am I envious? she wondered.

'Well, that was nice,' she said when he dropped her at her cottage.

'Most enjoyable. We must repeat it sometime.'

She said goodnight and went in. I've got it, she thought. I'm lacking in sex appeal. Somewhere there was, or had been, a man for her. Had it been Gavin? Had she made a mistake right at the beginning of her life? Never mind, she still had something: her writing.

She went upstairs to her computer and read what she had written. What became blindingly apparent to her was that she had lacked love in her early life with her mother, and it had made her unable to contemplate life with Gavin. She had run away from him to London, instead of grasping a future with him with both hands, then wasted her time with other men. Jan had warned her. But look at Jan! She was hardly a shining example. Yes, she was. She had had a happily married life with Joe, and had two daughters to show for it. Love was the important thing, Kate thought. A partnership that was not based on love was no partnership at all. She was sure from her memories of her father that he had been a loveable man, but her mother? Her behaviour towards her children had not shown love. She had been a self-centred woman, unable to give love. Had she, Kate, been the unlucky one, most affected by this? What kind of relationship had it been between her mother and her father?

Robert and Anne were walking by the river. She looked adorable, he thought. Her white dress contrasted with her faintly olive skin, and she was carrying a straw hat trimmed with pink ribbon. 'I like to see your hair,' he said, and teasingly, 'Is that why you always carry your hat?'

'I've been told it's my crowning glory,' she said, running her hand through its rich darkness.

'Who told you?' he asked. 'George?'

She stopped and turned towards him. 'I told you, George will never marry me.'

He put his arms round her and drew her towards him. 'I never know whether to believe you or not. There's only one way to prove it. Come away with me, and we'll get married.'

She put her arms round his neck. 'Where shall we go? Abroad somewhere? You've been all over, you lucky thing, and you've been left money now to indulge yourself.'

'I've told you before, Anne, that money is to buy a part of the farm and go in with George.'

'And I've told you before, Robert, if you do that, you lose me. You have to choose now: it's me, or George. I'll go away. I can't go on at home any more, that woman in the house and Father who is rarely home. Do you know what I think? He's got a woman in Glasgow!'

105

'*Your father is well thought of in the village. That's not true.*'

'*You don't know half of my life at home. I've never known a mother. We've been kept apart since I was a child.*'

'*I'm sorry for you, Anne darling, really I am. But you and I could have a happy home together, children you could love. What do you say? I love my brother too. Let's be frank with him and tell him we intend to marry.*'

*He watched the face he loved change. She was a difficult girl, Anne, he'd never known anyone like her. Sometimes loving, sometimes remote. Sunshine and shadow. '*I could show you love, Anne, real love.*' He bent to her face, which was held up to his, and kissed her passionately, again and again. When he released her, she was panting.*

'*Oh, Robert, I do love you. Stop! People will see us.*' *She took his hand and led him into the grove of trees at the side of the road.*

'*You're wicked,*' *he said. His blood was on fire. He caught her round the waist, and they fell on to the grass. They were laughing as they lay, side by side. His longing for her made him turn and lie on top of her. '*You've got to promise that you'll marry me. I'll tell George.*'

He knew she was a destroyer as he spoke. If they married, gone were his old days with George, the fun they'd had, they would never come again. In taking her, he was giving up his brother. Had George been wise in not marrying her? But he could not endure this passion for her. It was more important than anything else. Her arms went round his neck pulling him close, closer. A flashing picture seemed to pass before his eyes, George pulling him out of the Morris, and the two of them staggering along the path, laughing, he in his dripping clothes, weak with laughter . . .

As they walked back to the farm, she said, 'Yes, Robert, I feel like you. There's something special between us. You tell George tonight and I'll go to Glasgow with you. I couldn't live without you.' Her eyes were gleaming, silver.

Despite his joy, something inside George spoke to him. You're making a terrible mistake. What was it that was so strange about her? Those swift changes of facial expression, as if she was blown by the wind. The word is 'steadfast', he thought. She's not steadfast. George was, but would he ever forgive him?

'A penny for your thoughts.' There she was, facing him, pulling on her hat and hiding that luxuriant hair.

'I'm looking forward to the future with you, my darling.' He felt solemn, knew he must look solemn.

'You're such a serious man,' she said, covering his face with little kisses. 'You go on and tell your brother.' She walked away from him.

When he went into the farm kitchen George was there. And Isobel. 'Have you been having another swim in the Morris?' Isobel asked him. She and George were laughing.

His temper flared. 'Probably the last one I'll have.' He looked at Isobel. 'What I'm going to say, Isobel, is private.'

'Oh, I'm sorry if I'm intruding. Sorry if I've offended you.' She left the room and he heard her footsteps on the stairs.

'You're a bit short-tempered today, Rob.' It was George's pet name for his brother.

'Maybe I am. George, I've decided I can't come in with you.' He saw George's jaw drop.

'What about your Aberdeen Angus? God –' he put his hand to his forehead – 'what am I saying?'

'You can have them. And any calves that arrive.'
They both tittered.
'We'll talk about that later. I always hoped . . . it's that girl, isn't it?'
'I have to decide between you and her.'
To Robert's surprise, George extended his hand over the table towards him, palm upward. *'I wanted you in with me, not your money. Are you quite sure about Anne? You really love her? She's not bewitching you? You and I have been alike with women, treating it as a game. But this is different. She is different. I could tell you—'*
'I'm not a callow youth, George. Don't play the big brother with me.'
Isobel was at the door. *'Have you two settled the world?'*
'Come in, nosy,' Robert said. 'Maybe you'll wish me all the best. Anne and I are getting married.'
Isobel looked from one to the other. *'Is this true, George?'*
'Yes, he's a grown man. Everyone is entitled to settle their own future.'
'So that's that, Isobel. I appoint you to look after my Aberdeen Angus.' Robert felt his throat roughen.
'Oh, Robert!' She ran to him, and he put his arms round her. *'You're sure Anne hasn't put you up to this?'*
'Sure as hell,' he said. He looked round the kitchen and then at his brother and sister, feeling a pain he had never felt before, even when he was in the army and far away. *'I'll go and help Old Bob with the cows.'*
He walked out.

Ten

K ate typed until 2 a.m., unravelling her own life while writing about her father's. He had been ready to love, Kate thought, but he had married a woman who had been in love with someone else. She glanced at the mahogany clock on the mantelpiece. 'Presented by a few friends on the occasion of his marriage'. He had made the wrong choice.

Jan arrived the following morning looking beautiful with that air of fragility that was so appealing. She was wearing a black trouser suit, and her bleached hair stood out against it.

Kate welcomed her with genuine pleasure. 'You don't look like a jilted woman,' she said.

'No, I've taken myself in hand, decided there are better fish in the sea.'

'So you haven't given up on pairing?'

'No, the house is so damned quiet and tidy.'

'I like tidiness, I dislike other people's mess.'

'Is that a warning? I'll be an exemplary house guest, I assure you.'

'That was tactless. I like someone to cook for, but meantime let's have a cup of coffee.'

They sat until lunchtime, happy in each other's company. Kate told Jan more about the village and its inhabitants, especially about the elderly twins.

'They sound spooky,' Jan said. 'But this Mark, is he making a pass at you?'

'I don't think so. There's little or no rapport. I think at first I seemed the answer to his loneliness. On the face of it, it seemed possible, but, no, not for me. We weren't comfortable with each other.' Was it Kate's imagination or did Jan perk up?

'Do you remember the Hare and Hounds where we went the last time you came here?'

'Yes.'

'Mark took me there for a drink last night, and I asked the owner of the pub, Judy Grantham, to come here and meet you. Shall I phone her?'

'Why not? I'll have a look round your garden while you do it.'

It was Cyril who answered the telephone. 'Kate,' he said, 'the woman who holds her cards close to her chest. Yes, Judy is around. I'll get her for you.'

She came to the telephone. 'Hello, there.'

'Judy, my friend is here from London possibly for the weekend. How about coming to me for tea to meet her?'

'Oh, I should have liked that, but I have to look in at Lansdown Manor around five. Could I drop in on you before that?'

'Come for a snack lunch then, and it will give you more time.'

'OK.'

They had an enjoyable lunch together. Judy and Jan seemed to click. 'You breathe London to me,' Judy said to her. 'I never thought I'd miss it so much. My father died suddenly and left the pub to me, I'm the only child, and my mother died shortly afterwards. Everything happened in a rush. I met Cyril, and he was willing to come in with me, and so we landed here. I had been working in London.'

'I quite envy Kate here,' Jan said. 'She's settled down very well.'

'There's no doubt,' Judy said. 'Village life gives you a backbone. By the way, would you like to go with me to

Lansdown Manor? I phoned Sonia, who is by way of being the caretaker, and she said you'd be very welcome.'

'That's very kind,' Kate said, looking at Jan. 'Would you like to go, Jan?'

'Very much. Is it near here?' She spoke to Judy.

'Yes, just past Lansdown Lane. You know it, Kate – Mark Leaver lives down there.' Was there an undue emphasis on his name?

'Oh, yes, I know it. There's a stone wall bordering the lane. I thought it might be the grounds of some big house. Is that Lansdown Manor?'

'Right. Sonia Leroy lives there with Josh and Miriam Constantine. He is a film director and travels a lot, and Sonia is Miriam's sister. She was invited to live with them when her husband died, and she looks after the place while they're away. They're well-liked in the village. Give lovely parties.'

'We could walk back, Judy,' Kate said when they were leaving the cottage.

'We'll see.'

They got into Judy's car, and she drove them down the main road through the village and past the shops. She stopped at large ornamental gates just past Lansdown Lane, got out and spoke into the intercom. In a moment or two the gates swung open, and Judy drove through, up a gravel drive, stopping at an impressive doorway, with steps leading up to it, flanked by stone pillars.

The three of them got out of the car just as the door was opened by a middle-aged woman. She called from the doorway, 'Come along, Judy. And you've brought your friends?'

'Yes. You said you wouldn't mind.'

'I don't.' She was smiling, welcoming, a handsome woman with black hair drawn back from her face, which was pale-complexioned. She looked Italian, Kate thought, but Madame Leroy? French, surely?

She led them into a large drawing room where the sofas and chairs were covered with sheets. The furniture was handsome, with a Bechstein piano in one corner. 'I know you won't mind,' she said, 'but Josh likes this room used. Judy didn't give me time to prepare it. Please sit down.'

'It's a lovely room,' Jan said. 'You could get my whole house into it.'

'Yes, it's lovely,' Kate said, 'and what a beautiful view.' Outside the huge windows was a long terrace furnished with stone seats and carved urns, filled with geraniums, and beyond that was an expanse of lawn. In the centre was a pond with a double fountain spouting water from the centre.

'I have to turn on the water daily to check that fountain,' Madame Leroy said. 'Once Josh and Miriam came back, and the water refused to run. The fountain had got clogged. Could I get you some tea? We could go to my sitting room. It's much more comfortable.'

'No, thanks,' Judy said. 'We've just come from lunch at Kate's. But they'd love to see the garden, I know.'

'Of course. We could have a drink before you leave. I'll come with you. I could do with a breath of air.'

The comparison between the Blues' garden and this one was striking, Kate thought.

'I've seen another garden recently,' she said to Madame Leroy, as she was showing them round. 'But it was a far cry from this. It's so beautifully laid out, and planned.'

'That's my work,' Madame Leroy said, surprising Kate. 'Miriam is my sister, and when my husband died, they offered me a home here. I had designed our own garden in France, in Normandy, and they gave me carte blanche here. It's very French, I'm afraid – perhaps too formal for English tastes – but Miriam and Josh are quite happy with it. Josh calls it my Versailles.' She laughed.

'The garden I was referring to was the Blues' in Nettlebed Lane. They could do with your gardener,' Kate said.

'I have John Craig from the council estate. But I work

with him, you understand? I have thought of recommending John to them when Edna phones me, but she's rather strange. She phoned here when Josh and Miriam had gone to Italy where he was filming – they had just moved in – and she said she wanted to welcome them to the village, as her father would have done. Apparently he used to visit here when it belonged to Lord and Lady Lansdown, and she thought the connection ought to be kept up. "I am deputizing for him," she said. Josh, who is the soul of kindness, got Miriam to ring and invite them here, but Edna refused. "It is my place," she said. He says they need company. Miriam, who has also invited them, says she can't make head nor tail of them, but there you are. We're quite perturbed about them. It's a pity Dr Paxton died. He could have kept an eye on them.'

'I think Barbara Dexter drops in occasionally,' Kate said.

'That woman has a lot to do. The vicar doesn't visit and she takes his place. John Craig says people have become very disappointed in him. And they're worried about the twins. They have been heard at nights, in their garden, talking loudly to each other.'

'Why shouldn't they do what they like in their own garden?' Judy said. 'But that's typical of village gossip.' She looked at her watch. 'I'm afraid we'll have to forgo your offer of a drink, Sonia. Cyril gets agitated if I'm away too long. Would you like me to do any shopping for you? I'll be going to Leeston tomorrow. It's market day.'

'That's kind. May I phone you if I think of anything, Judy?'

They said goodbye to Madame Leroy, who extended an invitation to Kate to bring Jan again when she was in Mellor. When Judy drove them out, through the gates into the main road, Kate said, 'We'll get out here and walk back. You're in a hurry.'

'Well, that will suit me if you're sure.' They said goodbye with grateful thanks.

When they got to the corner of Lansdown Lane, Kate said, 'There are some lovely houses down there. Modern.'
'Shall we walk down and see them?'
'OK.'
When they passed Lorna Crook's house, Kate said, 'I've been in that one. A nice young couple.' She glanced at Mark Leaver's nursery and saw him driving out of the gate. 'Gosh, here's Mark Leaver.' He saw them and stopped the car. 'Hello there,' he said to Kate, 'you weren't coming to buy some plants, were you?' She saw his eyes went to Jan.
'No, I was showing Jan the very desirable residences down here.'
'Not mine. Can I give you a lift?'
'We're really out for a walk,' Kate said. 'Judy Grantham took us to see Lansdown Manor. That's why we happen to be in your vicinity. What do you think, Jan, do you want a lift?'
'It depends where you're going.' She looked at Mark.
'I was dashing to the shop. I had run out of bread.'
'Well, why not?' Jan looked at Kate. 'We'll walk from there.'
'OK,' Kate agreed reluctantly. They got into the back of the car, and in a minute or two they were at the shop. 'I'll run you back home,' Mark said, turning to them in the back.
'No, thanks,' Kate said. 'Jan's here on a walking holiday.'
They got out of the car, and expressed their thanks.
'I'll have to dash,' Mark said, 'they shut at six. Nice to see you again,' he said to Jan. Kate thought his eyes lingered on her. 'Enjoy your walking holiday with Kate.'
'I thought we'd better get out there,' Kate said to Jan. 'I didn't want to ask him in for a drink.'
'He seems very nice,' Jan said.

Kate said goodbye to her friend on the morning of the WI meeting. Jan had decided to go back to London that morning.

She set out at five to two on Tuesday afternoon for the village hall. The door was open and there was a woman at the piano. 'Hello,' she said, 'can I help you?'

'I have to meet Barbara Dexter here at two.'

'Oh, yes, you're Kate Armitage. She told me you were coming. She's through that door with Mabel.' She waved her hand. 'I'm just making sure I've got "Jerusalem" handy.'

'Oh, yes.' Kate smiled, repeating to herself, 'Got "Jerusalem" handy . . .' What have I let myself in for?

She was introduced to Mabel Rossiter by Barbara, and given her instructions about meeting Lia Dunn, the American woman who was their next speaker. She promised she would be at Leeston station with the car to pick her up. Lia Dunn would have a rose in her buttonhole. Barbara persuaded Kate to stay on for the meeting. By this time she was surrounded by members and it would have been difficult to refuse.

She found herself listening with assumed interest to a talk by a woman who was passionate about lacemaking, and wished to share this passion with her audience. As someone who had no interest in lacemaking, Kate put on an attentive face, and let her mind wander behind it. Her attention was drawn to the window, where three cows were gazing in with interest. If Jan were here she would have made a joke about that, she thought. 'Prospective members?' she might have asked.

Once the woman had finished her dissertation and answered questions about the art, there was tea and cakes. Kate was introduced to some of the members by Mabel Rossiter, who had taken her in hand, and was astonished at the politeness of the members. In the office, that virtue had been largely missing, and she thought, Well, they've got all the time in the world to be polite to each other. The pace here is slower. Shall I become like that trio of cows, bovine-faced? Do I like it? she asked herself. Time would tell. And then she remembered her writing. That was important to her.

115

She was taken to see the crèche, and met Lorna Crook there, who was in charge. Seb was playing with bricks, and Kate spent some time helping him in building a castle. 'I've fallen for Seb,' she said to his mother. If he were mine, she thought, I'd love him and love him.

Before long, Kate plunged into a routine, rising early, whizzing around doing housework, then after lunch she went upstairs to her study. Sometimes she sat there, letting her mind go back to her early years living with her mother. There was little joy in those memories. Her brother and sister had had little rapport with her because of the difference in their ages. Then she would think of Gavin, and how she had known joy in his company. She would close her eyes and think of the completeness of her life then, until he began to press her to get married. And how she had run away to London. And into the arms of John Newton, after a few affairs with younger men, all of which had been mistakes. Had she encouraged him because she missed Gavin so much, and because she knew he wouldn't want marriage? She had soon realized that the affairs with other men had been because the freedom of life in London had gone to her head, and because they didn't necessarily end in marriage.

Why did she avoid it? Was it the memory of that scene in the bedroom, with her mother weeping and her father comforting her, a scene that she hadn't understood? Had writing this book given her the answer? Or the courage to confront her demons?

Eleven

Kate had met Lia Dunn as arranged. She had had no difficulty in spotting her on Leeston platform, a tall girl with long fair hair, wearing a beige trouser suit with beige leather shoes and handbag, and a pink-toned Hermes scarf to match her pink rose buttonhole. They had an instant rapport. Lia was pleased with her reception at the village hall (she had confided to Kate that she was nervous about speaking to 'English ladies'), and when Kate drove her to Leeston station afterwards, they made an arrangement to meet in town.

It was now November, and Kate was slogging away at her book. Barbara Dexter and Ruth Paxton often came in for coffee, and Kate was a little surprised to discover she welcomed these interruptions. 'She has a hard time of it,' Ruth said, referring to Barbara Dexter, and Kate had asked them to drop in on her at any time.

'She's the only one I know who seems quite contented with her lot, despite her husband being so taciturn,' Ruth said. On one occasion, Barbara told them that she had had a letter from the school in Sussex, saying that they had a place for Belle after the Christmas holidays.

'You would think she would have been delighted,' Barbara said, 'but she's now saying she doesn't want to go. Ralph gets cross when she says this. I think he wants rid of the responsibility of her.'

'It's what she needs,' Ruth said once when Barbara had dashed away on one of her numerous errands. 'I've noticed

117

recently that Belle's quite "pert" – that's the only word I can use to describe her – as if she had something up her sleeve.'

Kate's life was sorting itself out. She was going up to town most weeks to meet Jan or Lia, as a break from village life, and writing in between. A nice mix, she told herself. Jan seemed to have perked up and was almost back to normal. Strangely enough, Kate hadn't seen or heard from Mark Leaver . . .

On one occasion when she was lunching with Jan, her friend surprised Kate by telling her she had met Mark occasionally in town.

'Did he phone you?' Kate asked, surprised at her own reaction.

'No, I phoned him to ask his advice about growing auriculas. We seemed to click. We've met several times and he's visited me at Streatham.' She looked embarrassed. 'You had said you found him difficult, but we get on very well. Oh, Kate, I don't know how to say this, but he wants me to shack up with him at Mellor. I think we could be really happy together, but I don't want to tread on your toes.'

'I'm flabbergasted, Jan,' Kate said. 'Needless to say I would love you to move to Mellor. But I think you might have told me you were seeing him.'

She was surprised at her own chagrin. Surely she wasn't jealous of her best friend? 'You've quite taken my breath away, Jan. I think I'm envious.' At her friend's concerned expression, she clarified: 'Not about you and Mark – I never was on any romantic footing with him.'

'The trouble with you, Kate, is that you analyze every relationship you're in. I see good points in every man I've lived with, I don't go looking for faults. Joe and I had an idyllic relationship, especially with the two girls. Before they came when we lived in New York, we had such fun.

'We were both fond of cooking, we even had two cookers, his and hers, and we threw wonderful parties. Then we came back to London, and it was much more sedate. I was busy with the babies and my job, and then Joe being ill, and dying, and I seemed to emerge at last from a long, dark tunnel. Then Nick came along and he gave me the fun I missed and now it seems that Mark and I have reached the same stage together – but not at your expense, I hope.'

'No, I'm glad for you and Mark. You've both got what you want, and I'm happy for you.' She put her hand on Jan's. 'Truly.' And she was a little surprised to realize that she was telling the truth.

It seemed, Kate thought later, that marriage wasn't the state of bliss that Jan purported it to be. She thought of Lorna Crook, dissatisfied with child-rearing and anxious to get back to work, and Barbara Dexter, who never complained but obviously didn't get the support she craved from her husband. Then there was Judy Grantham, who mothered Cyril. Jan seemed to be the only one who was happy, either with a husband, or a partner. Was adaptability the answer?

Now, in her cottage, Kate had time to think, to write, to put some of her thoughts into writing – not to regret Gavin, but to regret the time she had spent with John Newton. She was happy here, as she had never been in London. Occasionally she saw Jan when she stayed with Mark Leaver, and that Kate accepted, though it was strange knowing her best friend was just down the road with the man whose clumsy advances towards Kate could still make her blush if she let herself think about it. But she had never really regarded him as a possible partner, and evidently neither had he regarded her in that way.

She became involved in village life, she did duty at the crèche, she played bridge with some of the older people, in the stone houses of the village. She saw herself slotting into a way of life that satisfied her. She joined an art appreciation class in Leeston, and frequently went up to town either with them to visit galleries, or on her own. There were two invitations on her mantelpiece, one from the Constantines of Lansdown Manor for a Christmas party, and one from the American Embassy to a party as a guest of Lia and her husband.

It was the middle of November, the weather was wet and gloomy, and Kate spent more and more time at her computer upstairs, with the promised bright little fire. She felt she had learned a lot by finding out about her parents. It had helped her to understand herself, that there must be something of them in her, but that they could not be blamed for any mistakes she had made.

She became aware of nature, living in the village, as she had never been in London; she watched the dying down of trees and flowers in her garden, but she often walked across the Green to enjoy distant views. Space became important to her, she saw the contours of the village more clearly, now that it was stripped of foliage. It would be February before there were any signs of growth. Meantime the tall limes round the Hare and Hounds and the branches topping the wall at Lansdown Manor waved and shivered in the wind. Occasionally she had visits from Jan and Mark, and was glad to see them so happy and to know that there was no awkwardness between them all. Jan was contemplating selling her house in Streatham, but was hesitating. She had to consult her daughters.

The day of the Constantines' party came. It was talked about in the village shop as a landmark, and those who had had an invitation were much envied, although there were very few left out. The vicar and his wife had been invited, as the church choir would be singing Christmas hymns.

Kate was upstairs laying out her dress on the night in question. She had bought a new one in London for the occasion, and was contemplating whether or not it was too sophisticated. She had just decided that it was right for the occasion, when she heard the loud ring of her front doorbell. It had an imperious sound, and she ran downstairs, opened the door and found Ruth Paxton there, looking agitated.

'Oh, I'm not ready, Ruth,' she said. 'Give me . . .' They had arranged to go together.

'Nor am I. I had to come and tell you . . . May I come in?' Kate held the door open for her. 'Come into the sitting room,' she said. And when she had sat Ruth down, she said, 'What is it, Ruth? Something has happened . . .? Would you like a drink?'

Ruth waved her hand in dismissal. 'No, thanks. It's terrible. I've just had a phone call from Barbara. Belle has disappeared. They've called in the police.'

'The police!' Kate was horrified. 'What do they think?'

'She says Ralph insisted. He blames himself. Apparently he had a set-to with Belle this morning. They had had Garry Fox working in the garden during the week, and he reprimanded her for being "too familiar" with him. A row flared up and she flounced out of the house. Barbara says she has been rebellious since the date of her going to the school at Sussex drew nearer.'

'So, the police will question Ralph and Barbara before they start on their search. And Garry Fox's name will come up?'

'You're right.' She looked at Kate. 'There's no doubt she was fascinated by him.'

Kate thought of the night she had been with Mark Leaver in his car, and how she had thought the couple walking in front of them had been Belle and Garry Fox. And how she had buried the suspicion, because Mark had thought it was so unlikely. Should she confide in Ruth, or wait?

'Is there anything we can do, Ruth?'

'I don't think there is. Barbara says we should go on to the Constantines' and they will come along if everything turns out all right. She's an unfailing optimist, Barbara. Terribly clever, but quite unable to see the wood for the trees. For myself, although I never had any children, I should be terrified if I were in her shoes, human nature being what it is.'

'All right. We'll go on. I'll nip upstairs and get into my glad rags, and I'll be down in two ticks.'

'And I'll go and do the same and get my car out. We must go through the motions.'

'Yes, keep the flag flying.'

Kate flew upstairs and dressed hurriedly – it no longer mattered what she should wear – then checked herself, and going to her jewel box, selected her favourite pearls. It *was* Belle that night, she said to herself. She could quite easily slip out from that old house without her parents being aware of it. A typical teenager, Belle, she thought, even in this quiet backwater.

In half an hour, Ruth was driving them through the gates of Lansdown Manor. 'The Constantines have gone to town as usual,' she said. 'Look at this!'

'A winter wonderland,' Kate agreed. The trees sparkled with tiny lights. Around the pool with the fountain the grass was snowy, with imitation snow, and a huge snowman sat on it, complete with scarf and pipe. Christmas songs were being relaid by loud speakers.

The door was opened by Sonia Leroy, and Kate saw who she supposed were her sister and brother-in-law standing in the hall amongst a crowd of people. When Madame Leroy took Kate and Ruth to meet them, the warm welcome they received was indicative of a couple who were used to living in the limelight. 'Welcome! Ruth, we know, but you didn't tell us, Sonia, about Miss Armitage. A delightful addition to our friends in Mellor, don't you think so, Miriam?' Josh Constantine was portly, short and smiling. He seemed to Kate to be a man used to dealing with people. His eyes were sharp.

'Kate used to live in London, Josh,' his sister-in-law said. 'Judy Grantham brought her here while you were away.

Judy tells me that she's become part of the village already.'
'I'm so glad you were able to come,' Mrs Constantine said.
'We missed having our usual midsummer party by being in
Italy, but we do like to keep in touch with the village.'
'Have you heard from Barbara Dexter?' Ruth asked her.
'Yes,' she put her hand to her mouth. 'Dreadful! Let's
hope that everything turns out all right for them.' Her large
black eyes were full of sympathy. 'They'll come along later
if it does. Meantime we'll keep the news to ourselves?' She
looked questioningly at Ruth and Kate, and they both
nodded.

In no time, armed with a glass of champagne, Kate found
herself circulating in the hall. There was a fair sprinkling
of people whom she knew or recognized, and some she
didn't, presumably the owners' friends from London. She
stopped to speak to Mark and Jan. 'You and I were lucky
to be put on the list, Jan,' she said, 'being newcomers.'

'Yes, although I don't know if it's because of our previous
visit with Judy Grantham, or that I know Mark.'

He put an arm around her shoulders. 'It's because of me,
sweetie. My invitation said "Mr Leaver and friend".'

No, Kate thought, I'm glad it's not me. Jan can cope with
all that touching in public. Jan was smiling up at him, with
a look of bliss on her face.

'There are the choristers,' Kate said, as the choir burst
into 'Silent Night'. The lights were dimmed appropriately
and everyone stopped talking. Kate thought of the Dexters'
agony. She looked around. There was no sign of them. Had
Belle run away with Garry Fox? she wondered. Tomorrow
the police would be searching for him, questioning people,
scouring the countryside. Would they suspend operations
until tomorrow when it was light?

Mark said, when the choir had finished, 'I don't see the
Dexters here. They were coming, I know. Come and we'll
have a word with Judy and Cyril, darling.' He whisked her
away, saying to Kate, 'See you.'

She set off to look for Ruth, to see if she had any news. She found her talking to Josh Constantine. When she joined them, Ruth said to her, 'We're talking of Belle. Her parents haven't turned up.' Kate looked at their host. A man who was used to dealing with any emergency. A film director. He would be making something of the Dexters' dilemma already, picturing any possibility.

'I can see you two ladies are very worried,' he said. 'From my experience, one thinks of two things, a willing or unwilling disappearance. Both give one hope that she is at least alive. Why don't you come to my study and you could ring the vicarage?'

'That would set our minds at rest.' Ruth looked gratefully at him.

'Come along then, ladies.' He led them through the house to his study, showed Ruth the telephone, and said to Kate, 'Please sit down.' He sat opposite her and put his clasped hands between his knees. Together they listened to Ruth.

'Hello, hello, is that you, Barbara? It's Ruth. Have the police gone?' There was a pause while she listened. 'Yes, yes, start in the morning when it's light.' There was a longer pause. Kate looked at Josh Constantine. He returned her look. After a long time she heard Ruth say, 'I'll make your apologies, and Kate and I will drive round to see you.'

She looked at Kate, her eyebrows raised. Kate nodded. When she had hung up, Ruth said to Josh Constantine, 'Thank you. Barbara sends her apologies. The police are starting a wide scale search tomorrow. They don't feel they can come tonight. They have to stay put.'

'I quite understand. What a terrible situation for them. They'll be glad of your company.'

'We're sorry to miss the rest of the party,' Kate said.

'We'll slip away from here.' Ruth got up. 'Let's hope we meet again in happier circumstances.'

They left him at the back door, which led directly to where Ruth had parked the car. Josh Constantine looked concerned as they left him. A minute later Kate heard him say in a cheerful voice as he went back into the hall, 'Supper is being served, folks! Please make your way to the dining room.' A man who was used to dealing with any emergency.

Barbara greeted them at the door of the vicarage. She looked waif-like, Kate thought. Her hair, which was usually pinned up, was hanging round her face, which was tear-stained. 'Oh, you're good to come! Ralph was feeling so bad that he's retired to bed, but I've stayed up in case the phone rings . . . or she comes back . . .' She burst into tears and Ruth put her arms round her.

'You go into the kitchen, Kate, and make a cup of tea for us,' she said. 'Come, my pet, sit down on this sofa, you're worn out.' When Kate came back with a tray of tea things Ruth had persuaded Barbara to lie back on the sofa and put her feet up. She gave Kate a woe-begone smile.

'You're both so kind to me. But I must stay up in case the police phone.'

'Of course,' Kate said, thinking, Where the devil is her husband in all this?

'Did Jack Johnson come to see you?' Ruth said.

'Yes, it was he whom Ralph phoned when Belle . . . when it happened.'

'Jack was our local policeman,' Ruth explained to Kate. 'Then they built a spanking new police station on Mellor Road, on the outskirts of Leeston. It's supposed to serve all the villages around here as well as Leeston, and Jack was sent there.'

'He said he would keep in touch,' Barbara said.

The door opened and Ralph Dexter came in. He looked distraught. He nodded to Kate and Ruth.

'Any news?' he said to his wife.

'No. Kate and Ruth dropped by to find out. They were at the Constantines' party.'

'Oh, yes, we should have been there. How did the choir perform, Ruth?'

'Very well. Didn't they, Kate?'

'Oh, yes,' Kate said. 'Very well indeed.' There was an awkward pause. The man looked worse than his wife, haggard, eyes sunk deep in his face.

Ruth said, 'Well, now that the vicar is here, Barbara, we'll leave you. But we'll keep in touch. I'm sure things will turn out all right.'

'Do you think so? Thank you for dropping in. I'll phone you . . .' Her voice broke, and Kate saw that her husband went towards her and put an arm around her shoulders. Thank God for that, she thought. I hope he stays with her.

Ruth dropped Kate off at her cottage. 'You'll be feeling like me, Kate, exhausted. If I get any news I'll ring you.'

'I hope there is. It's terrible, isn't it?'

When she got into her own house, Kate went direct to the telephone. She asked to be put through to Mr Johnson.

'Inspector Johnson?' the man, presumably a policeman, said at the other end of the line. 'Can I take a message?'

'No, thank you,' Kate said. 'It's about the vicarage.'

'Oh, the disappearance of the daughter? I'll get him.'

In a few minutes she heard the inspector's voice in her ear. 'This is Inspector Johnson. Can I help you?'

'I hope so. I'm Kate Armitage. I live in Mellor, in Miss Thom's old cottage. You may remember her.'

'Indeed I do. How can I help you?'

'I know of Belle's disappearance. I've been there tonight. The thing is, Inspector, there's been something worrying me for some time. A month ago, I was being driven along Vicarage Lane at about twelve o'clock. Ahead of us there was a couple. We both recognized – or thought we recognized – Garry Fox as one of the couple. I thought the other person was Belle Dexter. Mark didn't think so. Mark Leaver – you know, he has a gardening business in Lansdown Lane.'

'Yes, I know Mark. But he didn't agree with you?'

'No, on the face of it, it was unlikely. As I said, it was

around twelve o'clock. Significantly they were walking *away* from the vicarage. Unless she had slipped out, I suppose it was unlikely to have been Belle. But I thought . . .'

'But you still think it was her? It's been bothering you?'

'I had decided to dismiss it from my mind, but now that Belle has disappeared . . .'

'Quite. I agree with you that it was perfectly possible for the young lady to slip out of her house and meet someone. Garry Fox is under suspicion of being that person, but I can tell you, Miss Armitage, since you have been frank with me, that we tried to interview Garry this evening, but his old mother said he had gone out, that he often did that late at night, and she knew better than to question him.'

'Well that's even more worrying,' Kate said, fear like a hand on her heart, squeezing it. 'That's the two of them missing.'

'We're not going to jump to any conclusions just yet, and neither should you, Miss Armitage. I'm telling you about Garry in confidence. We'll give him time, and see if he turns up tomorrow morning. There's a big scale search arranged for then.'

'Oh, that's good.' She wanted to say, 'Have you checked the trains at Leeston, or did Garry have a car, or was it missing?' She remembered when he and Mark had been working for her, Mark Leaver had arrived with Garry, but thought she might sound like Miss Marple. 'Goodnight, Inspector.'

'Good night, Miss Armitage,' he said. 'And thank you for getting in touch with me. Your information has been very valuable.' She hung up, shaking, but convinced she had done the right thing. Even so, she didn't like the feeling of having been an informer.

The next morning Kate was having breakfast when Inspector Johnson called round. She liked him. He seemed to her capable, and with a good knowledge of the village. 'I always liked these cottages,' he said, looking around. 'I've been calling on your neighbour, Mrs Paxton. Her husband and I were good friends. She knows the village thoroughly, having been the district nurse here. My men are going round the houses in Nettlebed Lane, and they are calling on houses round the Green. Then there's where Mark Leaver lives, at the other end of the village. It's amazing what one picks up.' His mobile rang. He cupped it in his hand, 'Yes?' He listened for a long time. 'You've made the necessary arrangements?' he asked. 'Yes, proceed. I'll be there in a few minutes.'

His face was stern as he raised it to Kate. 'A body has been found. I shall have to go to the vicarage. Do you know Mrs Dexter well enough to come along with me and support her?'

Oh, no, Kate thought, I'm not a member of the church. 'I should ask Ruth. She's known them for ages, and she would be upset if I went.' She watched Ruth a few minutes later, being helped into the inspector's car. Her face was suitably grave.

Kate waited at her window for what seemed like hours until she saw Ruth getting out of the inspector's car, and watched him drive away. After a few minutes she knocked on Ruth's door. Ruth opened it, eyes red. 'Come in,' she said.

Kate followed her into the kitchen. 'The inspector told me he was taking you to the vicarage. How did Barbara take it?' Ruth had collapsed on to a chair, her handkerchief to her eyes.

'How did Ralph take it, is more to the point. He needed help from above, that's for sure. Struck dumb. Poor souls.' She looked at Kate, her eyes streaming. 'Anyhow I went with them. It *was* Belle. They found her in the Nettlefields. I left with Jack, I felt they should be left alone. She had a bruise on her forehead. A doctor had been and pronounced her dead. Barbara was like a statue, then she flung herself down on Belle's body. Ralph knelt beside her with his arm round her shoulders. There were plenty of policemen around and Jack asked me if I'd like to be dropped home.' Her sobs, which she had restrained while she was speaking, now burst out, and Kate, saying to her, 'Cry it out, Ruth, it's terrible for you,' went about the kitchen making tea. She left her sipping from her cup. At least she had stopped the dreadful sobbing, which reminded Kate so horribly of her mother.

'I'll come in, later,' she said. 'You'll want to be alone.'

Ruth Paxton had had no children. She had been devoted to Belle.

Twelve

A pall seemed to hang over the village. Whispers circulated. When Kate had to go to the shop, she heard rumours. There had been a wide search over the village. People had been questioned. A new vicar took the Sunday service. Garry Fox had been taken away in a police van. When Kate knocked at Ruth's door there was no reply. She must be at the vicarage, Kate thought. Mark called to see her. Jan had gone back to London, temporarily.

'Do you think it was Garry Fox?' he asked her.

'Who knows?'

'There's a rumour going about that Belle was pregnant.'

'Oh, no!' Again she thought of the couple walking in the darkness, the man's arm around the girl's shoulders.

She tried to find consolation in her book, but found it had shrunk beside the real life tragedy all around her.

One evening when she was sitting staring at the computer screen, she heard her doorbell ring. When she rushed downstairs and opened the door, Ruth was standing there.

'You'll be wondering why you hadn't heard from me?' she said.

'Yes, but I knew you would be at the vicarage, and I didn't want to intrude. Have you time to come in?'

'Yes, I'd like to.'

'Come along, then.'

They settled down in the study, where Kate had been spending a lot of her time instead of downstairs in her sitting room. She kept a fire going, and she had installed

130

a sofa in front of it where she could lie and ponder on her book.

'This is cosy,' Ruth said.

'Yes, I've grown to like coming up here. Far from the madding crowd . . .'

Ruth laughed. 'There isn't much of that around here.'

'No. Everyone seems to have gone to ground.'

'I've been spending a lot of time with Barbara.'

'I guessed that. Is she coming to terms with . . .'

'Better than Ralph. I don't like to say this, Kate, but he hasn't much moral stamina. Of course there's a hiatus now, but Jack Johnson, who was a great friend of my husband's, keeps me informed. I'm the sieve.'

'Is Garry Fox still under suspicion? I shouldn't ask that.'

'Not for Belle's disappearance, but for child molesting. Belle was found to be three months pregnant.'

'I had heard a rumour. Poor little thing.'

'Had you guessed?'

'No. But once when I was being driven by Mark Leaver along Vicarage Lane, I thought I saw the two of them walking in front of us. Around twelve o'clock. I told Inspector Johnson.'

'Good for you.'

'In a way, Ruth, it was predictable, when you think of it. A nubile girl, with nothing much to occupy her. She would have been better off at Leeston Grammar.'

'Yes, I agree. The vicar is to blame there. It's terrible how epilepsy and other things like mental illness are regarded as shameful by some people. He simply hadn't come to terms with it. An only daughter, she had to be perfect in his eyes.'

'Yes. Do you know, Ruth, as you speak, I have a feeling that epilepsy is somehow at the root cause of her death.'

'Investigations are going on by cleverer brains than ours. I know they are combing the area around where she was found, interviewing people.'

'Do the twins know about Belle having been found in the Nettlefields?'

'I know Jack Johnson has been to see them once or twice. He says they are difficult to interview, but he knows them. He'll get them to talk, I'm sure.'

Kate thought long and hard about the elderly twins when Ruth had gone away. Edna had control over Eva. She could school her in what she had to say. But then she could break down under skilful questioning. How could they possibly be involved? she asked herself. Unless they had seen something? They were near the Nettlefields . . .

Then there was Garry Fox. If Belle told him she was pregnant, was he capable of killing her? From what she knew of him, she didn't think so. He didn't seem to her to be a violent character.

One evening, when she couldn't work, Kate got into her car and drove to the Hare and Hounds. If there was any gossip going around they would have heard it.

To her surprise when she pushed open the door, she saw Mark and Jan at the bar. 'Hello!' she said. 'I thought you were in London, Jan?'

'No, I've finally come back here – arrived this morning. We were going to pop round to your cottage and tell you. I've had a talk with the girls and I'm going to sell my house. Mark says he would be glad to have me.' The look they exchanged was definitely loving.

'That's marvellous,' Kate said. 'I'm so glad you're coming to live in Mellor.'

'She took a lot of persuading,' Mark said. 'And what's more we're going to be married.'

'That's marvellous! Well, that's made my day. It's been gloomy around here, hasn't it, Cyril?' He had joined them.

'You can say that again. Judy is going to have a notice printed for the counter: "Please don't ask us anything about the recent events in this village". One thing about it is, it has increased our custom no end. You'd be surprised at the number of people who come from near and far around, prying . . .'

'Have you any theories?' Mark asked.

'Well, if Garry Fox isn't the guilty party, and from all accounts, he might well be, I'm stumped. Certainly not the twins. They live in a fantasy world.'

'Unless they had a drunken orgy.' Judy had joined them. They all looked at her. She had her hand to her mouth.

'Steady on, sweetie,' Cyril said. 'That's ghoulish.'

Jan said, 'In London I get my kicks from the papers. Here it's on your doorstep. Mark tells me the girl was an epileptic. That's a frightening thing, if you're not used to it. I had a niece who was afflicted. I was visiting them once when Amanda . . . her family took it in their stride . . .'

Back home, Kate sat in her study, thinking of the Dexters. That poor girl. Barbara, should she call? She decided she would walk round to the vicarage tomorrow morning, and offer her sympathy at least. She was downstairs preparing her supper when her telephone rang. It was Ruth.

'Jack has called. It will hit the papers tomorrow, in a big way. Would you like me to come round?'

'Yes, Ruth. Come right away. I can give you supper if you haven't eaten.'

They sat for a long time in the kitchen over a bottle of red and ravioli. One always made enough for two, Kate assured Ruth as she served her with a generous portion.

'Garry is guilty of child molesting but not of murder. The twins have been interviewed several times, simply because they were near the Nettlefields where the body was found, and they might have heard something. They know Jack, and he paid several visits to them.'

'Softening-up process,' Kate said.

Ruth nodded. 'He said there were lots of bottles lying around. Eventually he succeeded in getting Eva to talk by taking her for a run in his car; she had dearly loved driving the family car when Colonel Blue was still alive. She said she was telling him in confidence what had happened and made him promise not to tell Edna. Eventually she came clean, during her third run in the car.'

'Do you think he let her drive?' Kate said.

'Kate!' Ruth pretended to be shocked.

The story that had emerged, chiefly from Eva, was surprising, but eventually had been corroborated by Edna, when she was told that Eva had confessed to Jack. Kate saw the scene unfolding before her as Ruth spoke.

'The twins were sitting in their drawing room, as they called it, with their morning sherry, when Belle arrived on the Sunday morning. She was agitated, saying she had to get away from Daddy. Suddenly she fell down, in a fit, striking her head on the side of the fender.' Kate remembered this as being a heavy, old-fashioned object with wooden seats at either end.

'She had struck her head on the corner of one of the seats, and her writhing and waving of hands had slowly stopped. Blood had run from the wound, and Edna had mopped it up with a napkin she had got from a drawer of the sideboard in the dining room. Then they had bound her forehead with another napkin. She had gradually stopped moving and she had gone very pale and cold.

'Eva had started to weep and Edna had told her to stop, and given her another sherry. She had to realize that Belle was dead, and they would be blamed for it. Then Edna had had a brilliant idea. They would wrap her in the white damask tablecloth that was still on the table in the dining room – it would look like a shroud – and then carry her through one of the holes in the wall into the Nettlefields and hide her in the remains of the gazebo there. "Don't you think that was brilliant, Jack?" Eva had asked him.'

'The damask would be a clue,' Kate said, 'if they had to verify her story. Not many people possess tablecloths like that.' Ruth agreed, and went on.

'They were both exhausted when they got back, but Edna

poured them a stiff glass of sherry each, and told Eva to keep quiet about what had happened. She had admitted that Belle had visited them on the morning in question, but had said she had gone away to meet Garry Fox.

'Oh, yes, they knew all about him. They had watched him in the Nettlefields with girls, often.'

'How terrible!' Kate said, shaking and horrified. 'Edna! She was evidently the ringleader.'

'Yes, but surprisingly, Edna herself told Jack what had happened, admitting that she had told Eva not to confess under questioning. Jack thought she was jealous of Eva going out with him in the car.'

Thwarted sex, Kate thought. There must be a name for it.

'Of course,' Ruth said, 'they're certifiable . . .'

'Poor things!' Kate said. 'They must have been terrified when they saw Belle falling to the floor, then the knock on her head, which presumably was the cause of her death. Funny that they had never seen her fitting before. She called on them often.'

Ruth shrugged. 'Could be the luck of the draw, but I suspect Belle didn't visit them as often as she said. They were a convenient alibi for her trysts with Garry Fox. Those on the case will work out time and cause of death . . . oh, they're clever now, and then there's DNA testing for Garry I presume . . . the thing is that perhaps Belle's life could have been saved, if they had alerted the police in time . . . Oh, it's horrible. I've been with the Dexters all this evening. Fortunately, Ralph has rallied and they're comforting each other, and the boys have been sent for. Thanks, Kate –' Kate had topped up her wine. 'If it's hard for us to bear, think of that poor family. I hope for their own sake they move away from this village. The diocese could find him another parish.'

Kate was silent. All life is here, she thought. Is it in my book? But no book could ever compare with this.

* * *

There was a huge turnout for Belle's funeral at the church. The young curate took the service, and the Constantines had the church decorated as there were no flowers to be had in the village gardens. It was a white bower of arum lilies and exotica. The service was simple, a memorial to Belle, and the vicar had invited several villagers to speak of their regard for the Dexter family. One elderly lady from the stone houses on the main road asked people to remember the Blue twins, who had formed such an integral part of the village. Ralph Dexter spoke of their loss and took the opportunity to say goodbye, as a new parish in the West Country had been found for them.

One of the Dexter sons drove their parents back to the vicarage, and Ruth and Kate organized tea for them and the young vicar and his wife. The Constantines offered Landsdown Manor, but it was felt that people had had enough opportunity in the church to express their sympathy.

When it was all over, and Kate had helped out at the vicarage, she drove home, thoroughly worn out. How must Barbara and Ralph Dexter feel? And Belle's two brothers? She didn't feel like speaking to anyone, and she knew Ruth would feel the same. She had been stalwart in her help to the Dexters. She had told Kate that her husband had attended Barbara at the birth of her three children, and she herself had always been available in her role as district nurse.

Sure of not being disturbed, Kate took herself off to bed. For once she had no desire to work on her book.

Thirteen

The shroud seemed to linger over the village despite Christmas. People went about with tight-lipped faces, determined not to discuss either the Dexters, the Blue twins or Garry Fox. Some gave in, as Kate was aware, by the small knots of women collected round the post office. The new vicar, Derek Strong, did his best by organizing cheerful evening services in the church, and his evident popularity did a great deal for the village. His young wife, equally cheerful, with two small children, was a decided asset. It was plain to see that they had set themselves the task of helping Mellor through a bad patch.

The Women's Institute gave a farewell party for Barbara Dexter, their president. Everyone admired her, because of how she had stood up to the loss of her daughter. That she had been deeply affected was plain to be seen by her haggard face and sunken eyes. Her smile remained, but it was at odds with her shattered appearance.

Kate had a talk with her before she left. 'We mustn't lose touch, Barbara,' she said. 'You were such a good friend to me when I came to Mellor. We could meet in town.'

'Well, Taunton isn't so far away. We'll keep in touch. You could come and visit when we get the vicarage put in order. It was an unmarried vicar who was in it before us, and I believe there's lots to be done. Oh, I'll miss Mellor.' She put her hand on Kate's. 'I was so happy here.'

'I know. Remember I'm always ready to help if . . . things get too much for you. Just ring me . . .'

'I'll do that.' Her sweet smile was heart-breaking to Kate. Is it a double loss for her? A daughter and a grandchild, or doesn't she allow herself to think like that? she wondered.

Slowly things returned to normal. There was a blanket of snow over the village early in January, and Kate decided not to drive up to town for the party at the American Embassy, but to take the train. Marylebone Road looked bleak and desolate, an after-Christmas look, and she hailed a taxi to take her to the hotel where she had booked a room for an overnight stay. There she dressed in her evening dress and set off for Grosvenor Square.

She was welcomed in the hallway by a man in court dress and presumably his wife, and then was claimed by Lia and her husband.

'Craig's dying to meet you,' Lia assured her.

'Hi, Kate!' he said. 'I've heard so much about you from Lia.'

They led her to a reception room buzzing with the voices of men and women in evening dress, and introduced her to a few of their friends. There was no trouble about knowing their names, as they uniformly greeted her by announcing their own. So different from English parties, she thought. There was no time to feel awkward or self-conscious for having come by herself.

She looked around, momentarily finding herself with a group of people who were laughing and talking – Craig and Lia had been whisked away – and her eyes fell on Gavin and her heart skipped a beat. He was smiling at her with Gavin's smile – older, of course, certainly fifty, in his prime, hair grey at the temples. Gavin's hair had been dark, but it had been cut in the same way, by a barber determined to subdue recalcitrant curls. Dark, thick eyebrows, good teeth (Gavin had been proud of his teeth – his father had been a dentist), and this man was tall, also like Gavin, with that same slight forward swagger as he pushed through the crowd towards her.

138

He bowed. 'Sandy Graham. I don't think we've been introduced,' he drawled.

'I don't think so. Kate Armitage,' she said, still reeling from the shock of his resemblance to Gavin.

'Kate Armitage,' he repeated, 'would you care to have this dance with me?' Of course, people were dancing in the next room. She heard the band, loud and brash, with a saxophone leading it in a slow melody as befitted the American Embassy.

'I haven't danced for ages,' Kate said, finding herself in Sandy Graham's arms. Yes, she had had to look up at Gavin, like this.

'I wouldn't have thought so,' he said, smiling down at her, with that curved-lip smile Gavin had had.

'Do you know,' she said, 'I've got to say it, you're remarkably like a man I used to know.'

'Was he American?'

'No, Scottish.'

'Every American wants to claim Scottish ancestry. What was his name?'

'Gavin Armstrong.'

'Armstrong . . .' he pondered. 'That name might well be on our family tree . . . yes, I'm sure it is.' His eyes were dancing. They were grey, flecked, seemingly with light.

'I'll believe you,' Kate said, 'thousands wouldn't.' It was a phrase she and Gavin had used.

'I'm generally a believable sort of guy.' His smile broadened. 'Let's get back to base. Do you live in London?'

'I used to. I moved to a little village when I retired.'

She saw his eyebrows raise. 'I'm looking for the grey hair. You did say "retired"?'

'I did. Voluntary retirement. But I had a longing for the country although all my life has been spent in towns.'

'I'm a country boy myself. Colorado. It's not often you find someone like me in the diplomatic service.'

'Were you brought up in Colorado?' She had a picture of bucking broncos.

'No, New York. Our home is there. The ranch in Colorado is my father's hobby.'

Kate choked back the words, 'Like George Bush.' Although this man seemed good-natured, she had to remember he might well be a Republican. She and Gavin had been politically-minded. For the people.

'You seem to have such an exotic background. Mine was very ordinary. I decided to go to London, was in a publishing firm. Then I retired.'

'Oh, have I been sounding off? Actually, the politics was due to my dad's influence. He was a self-made man. Built up a business in New York, then politics. Had great ambitions for his family, the usual story; they must have everything he hadn't had. I was sent to Harvard, and became politically minded there. I joined a debating society, and subsequently was picked for the Embassy. I've been with it ever since, and landed up in Grosvenor Square, after occasional postings to the trouble spots.'

She thought, He's been helped along all the time by a powerful father. I didn't have one to guide me. 'It's odd,' she said, 'to have two middle-aged people talking about their careers.'

The band had stopped, and still talking he led her into a corridor with huge sofas scattered about, his arm around her shoulders. They sat down on one of them. Kate had felt a tremor of excitement when he touched her, and silently chastised herself for behaving like a blushing schoolgirl.

'Do you ever get the feeling,' he said, 'that you can't possibly be the age you are? Ask yourself where the time has gone?'

'Often,' she said.

'Are you married?' Kate looked up and saw Craig and Lia standing there.

'Sorry to have deserted you,' Lia said, 'but I see you have been well looked after.'

'Yes.' Kate smiled at Sandy Graham. 'He's telling me all

about his background. I don't know whether to believe him or not.'

'You can,' Craig said. 'I've worked with him for a long time. I can vouch for him. He's a real cowboy.'

'Thanks, pal,' Sandy said. The quizzical upward smile at Craig reminded her so much of Gavin that her heart gave a wrench. 'I'll do the same for you sometime.' He got up and kissed Lia. 'Still my favourite girl.'

She laughed. 'Look out, Kate, he says that to all the women. We came to find you. Would you like to come with us and have some supper?'

'Yes, thanks.' She got up.

'We'll all go and have supper,' Sandy Graham said.

The next two hours was the best time Kate had had in a long time – definitely since she had lived in Mellor. She found that the sad events there were erased from her mind as the four of them talked and laughed, Sandy making her feel like the most beautiful, interesting woman in the room. The gaiety was infectious. In no time, it seemed, she found herself outside the Embassy with Sandy Graham, waiting for a taxi, wondering where the time had gone. Craig and Lia had said goodnight and left them.

'I could have run you home, if I'd known we were going to meet up,' Sandy Graham said, looking sideways at her, when they were both leaning back in the taxi.

'If ifs and ands were pots and pans . . .' she said.

'I've never met someone like you before,' he said. She felt his eyes on her, lingering. 'Kate, I have to fly back to New York tomorrow evening for a fortnight, business and pleasure. Could I persuade you to stay on in London tomorrow and have lunch with me? I feel we have so much to talk about.'

'Yes, I'm persuaded. Being retired I have no claims on my time. And I'm not married.' She saw a quick look of delight in his eyes as the taxi pulled up. 'Here we are,' she said.

'So we are. I'm so glad you're not married.' He was beaming as he helped her out. 'Neither am I. I'll pick you up tomorrow here at twelve. Is that OK?'

'OK,' she said.

His eyes held hers as they shook hands at the foot of the steps leading to the glass door of the hotel. Then he ducked forward and planted a kiss on her cheek, saluted and got back into the taxi. She stood watching him being driven away. A reincarnation of Gavin. Strange . . .

She thought she wouldn't sleep for thinking about him, but that must be the prerogative of young girls, she told herself. Often she had lain awake after a night with Gavin, reliving his love-making in his old banger. That had been her youth, now she was middle-aged. Would there no longer be such heights and depths?

Kate was told Sandy was in the lounge waiting for her, when she was upstairs wishing she had more clothes with her than a simple skirt and jersey.

She ran down the stairs like a young girl. Serve her right if she fell.

He was on his feet and coming towards the door when she pushed it open. It was weighted and he had to help her. 'It was scarcely worth all that effort,' he said, 'since we won't be sitting here. Let's get to the restaurant. When is your train?'

'Four o'clock.'

'Suits me. The place I've booked is near your station. Marylebone, isn't it?'

'Yes.'

'Right.' He took her case from her, put his arm around her shoulders and got her through the door. 'I've got a taxi waiting,' he said. He smiled at her, and to her dismay she felt herself blushing.

They talked and talked – in the restaurant she had heard about, but never been in, quietly elegant – questions and answers. She kept a discreet eye on her watch, and also the level of the fine Pouilly-Fuissé he had provided.

During a pause, a slight pause, she said, 'I was surprised you weren't married.'

'I was delighted you weren't married. I was – I'm divorced now. Sally and I had two children. Grown up now. Delia is married, two children also. I'm a grandfather. Does that appall you?'

'Not at all. You must be the age to have grandchildren.'

'I'm fifty. We were married very young, before we had any sense.'

'So am I – fifty . . . I wish I had grandchildren. Now that I'm too old to have children of my own, I have discovered a longing to cuddle any that come near me.' She thought of Seb.

'I'd like to tell you about Sally and I.' He paused, fingering his glass. 'As I said, we married young. I was too dull for her as I was studying during the early part of our marriage, and she found someone else to take her around. It was my fault.'

'Does it still worry you?'

He raised his eyebrows questioningly.

'I mean, that you neglected her?' Kate said, thinking, I would have stuck by him, but then reminded herself, You ditched Gavin.

'It did. But I now see it was a mismatch. But I'm sorry it deprived our children of a stable background.' He topped up her wine.

'Careful,' she said, 'or I'll miss my train.' She looked at her watch. Three thirty. 'We've got half an hour.' He nodded, summoned a waiter, signed the bill. 'I want you to think well of me,' he said. 'Shall we go? We can talk in the taxi.'

'Yes.' She took a last sip of her wine and stood up. He helped her on with her coat, which the waiter had brought (he must have been watching), and when they went out a taxi was waiting. Such service, she thought. But, of course, a place like that . . .

In the taxi she said, 'Thanks for a lovely meal, Sandy, in case I have to dash for my train.'

'It was my pleasure. I hope we'll have many more. Kate, I shall be back in a fortnight.' He took her hand. He wasn't smiling. 'I feel this is the start of something good. Do you feel the same?'

'Yes.' There was no point in prevaricating. That was the point of being fifty: one didn't.

They walked quickly to her train, and he saw her to her compartment. She put her case on an empty seat – there were two or three people seated already – and went back to the window. He was standing, waiting. 'We made it,' she said, smiling down at him.

'Yes.' He put his hands over hers. 'I hate to see you being taken away from me, just when we were getting to know each other.'

'Don't worry,' she said, 'there's plenty of time.' I wouldn't have said that thirty years ago, she thought. But when one is young everything is so urgent. It was such an apposite thought, that she repeated it. 'There's plenty of time.'

'I'll try not to get run over in New York,' he said, grinning at her.

She saw the train guard becoming galvanized and raising his flag. 'We're off,' she said. He looked round. 'You're off.' He tightened his grip on her hands. She bent down and touched his cheek with her lips. 'Goodbye,' she said. She felt like Celia Johnson in *Brief Encounter*, minus the hat. The train juddered, and began to move slowly away.

'I'll call you,' he said. 'Don't forget me.' He was walking quickly beside the train.

She shook her head, her eyes filling and left the window, sat down in her seat. Six pairs of eyes were on her. Act like a woman of fifty, she told herself. She unzipped her case and took out the novel she was reading, re-zipped it and got up to put it on the rack. A middle-aged gentleman was at her side, possibly about fifty. 'Allow me,' he said. She thought she saw understanding in his eyes.

When she opened her door and went into Rose Cottage, Kate felt a feeling of security, such as she had never known in her flat in London. She made a cup of tea and sat down to read her mail, mostly junk. There would be nothing from Barbara yet. She had a desire to know how the village had got on without her, and knew she wouldn't be able to settle to anything with all the butterflies in her stomach. She lifted the telephone and dialled Mark Leaver's number. 'Hello, Mark. It's Kate. Is Jan there?'

'Yes, she's in the kitchen.' Ministering to him, she thought. 'I'll get her. I believe you've been gallivanting up in town?'

'You could call it that.' Her voice was drowned by his loud bellow, '*Jan!*'

Jan was there. 'Kate! How did you get on?'

'It was a lovely party. Plenty of people – mostly American, as you would expect.' She hesitated, unsure whether to tell her friend all about the handsome stranger she had met.

'What are they like en masse?'

'Very friendly.' She suddenly didn't want to tell her about Sandy Graham. Maybe that was why she found herself here at fifty. 'I've been wondering if there have been any developments in the village about Belle . . .'

'Nothing specific. The vicar has told Martin that he's being allowed to visit the old ladies.'

'That's good. Nothing more in the papers?'

'You've only been away a night, Kate!'

'Yes, I know.' Jan hadn't developed Kate's feeling of belonging yet. But then, she had had a feeling of belonging for a long time, with a husband and children.

'Why not come down to the Hare and Hounds tomorrow night? We're going to drop in at around six. Judy and Cyril are becoming buddies.'

'Yes, I may do that. Bye – just wanted to touch base.' She hung up. She could imagine Jan's puzzled face.

The next few days Kate spent keeping herself busy, trying not to think about Sandy Graham. She met Mark and Jan in the pub, she did a stint at the crèche, and cuddled Seb, and received a visit from Liz Strong, the vicar's wife. She was a jolly girl, with a baby in a pusher and a toddler by her side, but obviously willing to play her part as the vicar's wife. 'I hope you get in touch with Lorna Crook,' Kate said. 'I'm sure you two would get on together, and you're at the same stage of baby-rearing.'

'Oh yes, we've met. We have a lot in common. But I'm trying to help Derek. Most people are shocked at the tragedy, but he's doing his best with counselling. He's dedicated, and so am I.'

'If I can help, let me know,' Kate assured her.

She took several walks around the village, and thought the roads were quieter than usual. The Strongs would find plenty to do in their ministry, and she tried to give a cheerful greeting to anyone she met as a contribution . . . To each their own, she decided and took herself up to her study. She found the book flowed more easily, and that the end was looming in front of her. Happy endings were out. So were cliff-hangers, but wasn't her life like that just now?

She felt settled with her life here. Did she want to disturb it with an affair? It would have to be more than that. Her affair with John Newton had done nothing for her in the event. After all, Sandy Graham had her telephone number. She conquered the desire to hang about the house waiting for his call.

Time went on. It was a week since she'd seen him. She tried not to feel disappointed that she hadn't heard from him. Ruth came in for coffee, and they had a long talk about the Blue twins. Eva was seriously ill, and they both looked, the vicar said, as if they were withering away. Events had proved too much for them. As for Garry Fox, the vicar had made an application to visit him in prison. Kate remembered a saying of her Scottish mother: 'A glutton for punishment.' Derek Strong could only be admired.

At the end of the second week when she had had no telephone call, Kate began reassuring herself. He had been busy, with diplomatic work and his family. She could be quite happy here if she never saw him again, couldn't she? She was a writer. She had to finish her book. Was there anything she had learned in writing it? Yes, there was. There was that wonderful memory of the party organized by her father to bring joy into their lives. He must have been thinking of his own happy life at the farm. There was the realization that her mother had been a deeply unhappy, troubled woman whose depression had tainted the lives of all those around her. And most importantly, the knowledge that Kate had held herself back, resisted love and happiness, but that it was time to move forward and accept responsibility for her own life and her own mistakes.

She went upstairs to her study, stoked the fire into a comforting blaze, and began. This was a good ending, she thought, happy, as she felt the remainder of her life was going to be. She had learned how to live.

Kate put a CD of her novel in an envelope and posted it to John Newton with a covering letter. 'Choose your own title. I thought of *The Learning Curve*.' The die is cast, she decided. If he takes it, I shall be able to call myself an author. An author living in her sylvan retreat. She could see the book jacket already.

Was she being honest with herself? 'Quite happy': would that suit her? Did she mind being alone? Becoming that well-known woman author Kate Armitage, living in Mellor.

People looking at her with new eyes. 'How do you do it? I aways feel I have a book inside me. But how do you get started? Of course, being unmarried you have plenty of time . . .'

Sandy, please come back to me. It's taken me a long time to learn – what was it that Jan said to me? 'The trouble with you is that you analyze every relationship you're in. I see good points in every man I've known.' Was it fear in Kate's case? If you grew up in an atmosphere of fear and mistrust it was bound to colour your outlook on people.

But the beauty of it was that when I met you, Sandy, I didn't have any doubts at all. This is it, I said to myself, triumphant. No doubts at all. I was being given a second chance, even someone who reminded me of Gavin. Someone more mature than Gavin, who had been 'through the whins', as my mother used to say. Right, just right. A promise of happiness, of growing old together, someone who was just right. If you don't come back, never come back, I'll . . . The bleakness of her future without him brought an unbearable pain to her heart. She got up and undressed, 'tears tripping her' – another saying of her mother's – and crawled into bed, where her sobbing could be indulged.

The following morning Kate had a call from Sandy Graham.

'Kate, how are you? I should have called you earlier. My poor father was ill when I arrived, and I travelled with him to Colorado, which he wished. We intended to have a family party at the ranch, but he had a severe stroke when we arrived. We all hung about for days while he hovered between life and death, my mother badly needed my support. I can't tell you what it was like, I had to get in touch with my sister and her family, and my own, and the attorney. Well, he died, and being the only son I had to hang around to take charge of arrangements, and the funeral. My sister is a widow, and I couldn't locate Peter, my son – I'll tell you about that later.'

She sat up in bed, feeling herself to be part of this Graham family. She could cuddle Delia's children, and maybe help with Peter, who obviously had problems of his own. She took a quivering breath, trying to hide her excitement. 'I'm so sorry about your father,' she said. 'Are you all right?' Stop feeling so happy, she told herself. This man's father has died. He was lucky to be around, though. She repeated this aloud. 'Wasn't it a good thing you were around?'

'I was hoping you'd say something like that. Well, all this has put things into perspective for me. Kate, I know it seems premature, but will you consider marrying me when I get back?' Her heart gave a jump at the words.

'Eventually. But I'd like to be wooed first.' She surprised herself by saying this.

'Oh, I'll woo you and woo you! Darling, I'm flying back to England tomorrow night. I'll come straight to you.'

'I can't believe this!' What had happened to all her reserve, her defences?

'Nor can I. Stay right where you are. I have your address, haven't I?'

'I think so. Phone me when you arrive in London and I'll give you directions.'

'I'll do that.'

'We're both being very calm. Do you feel calm?'

'I'm pretending to be calm.'

She sprang out of bed, her mind whirling, and began looking through her wardrobe, checking she had clean underwear and tights, putting clean sheets on the bed, laying out clean towels in the bathroom. Now she had a decent lot of washing and ironing to do. That would fill one day. And then there was her hair. She would drive into Leeston to that posh hairdresser's, 'Sue and Nicky', and have the whole cabosh, especially a rinse to bring out the copper glints in her hair. That was another day. She would have a dainty little lunch at Le Rendezvous, where all the elite from the surrounding villages met. She must keep herself busy, stop herself from panicking or coming up with all the reasons why she shouldn't let her heart run away with her head.

She was painting her nails when the telephone rang on he third day, and she ran towards it, shaking her wrists and lifting the receiver gingerly. 'Hello?' she said.

'Hello!' It was John Newton's voice. 'Kate, how are you?'

'I'm fine – great!'

'You sound it. Look, about—'

'Please, John, there's no need to explain. Things are better this way.'

'Thank God! Anyway, I'm calling in a professional capacity. It's about the book.'

'Oh, the book. What did you think of it?'

'Flabbergasted. Only one thing: the ending. I would like it to be more definitive.'

'Definitive? Yes, I think I'll be able to make it more definitive. But you like it?'

'It's terrific! I knew you could do it. I've already put it up at a meeting, and they all agree with me: a more definitive ending.'

'That shouldn't be difficult. Give me a few weeks.'

'You sound very positive.'

'I had two endings. I'll let you know soon which one pans out.'

'It may not hit the headlines, but it is every thinking person's idea of what a good book should be like.'

'Say no more, John. My head's spinning. I'll hang up now. I'm waiting for a phone call and I don't want to miss it.'

'OK. May I congratulate you, Kate. I must say I'm astounded, but I always knew you were special.'

'Thanks. How are things between you and your wife?'

'Good. We had a family holiday and did a lot of talking.'

'Oh, that pleases me. I'm so glad for you. I shall have to hang up, John. This call is important.'

'Fair enough. I think of you very fondly, Kate.'

'That's good to know.'

In a second or two the telephone rang. 'Kate, I couldn't get through to you. I was beginning to panic.'

'You shouldn't have worried. An old friend phoned me with some good news. Have you got a piece of paper?'

'Ready and waiting.' She gave him the instructions she had given to Jan. It seemed so long ago.

'I'm on my way,' he said.

She made herself sit down with a cup of coffee. This is a momentous morning, she told herself. My book is a success, and I'll see the man I love soon. She imagined him at the wheel of his car, bent over, speeding towards her, wearing a cowboy hat. Was that what she wanted, as well as her book? Yes, it was. She had only to imagine herself going on writing without him, and the prospect seemed dull indeed.

She rinsed the cup, prepared the percolator with fresh coffee, ran upstairs, sat down at her dressing table, made up her eyes, put on lipstick, brushed her hair and swept it up on top of her head, *à la* Sue and Nicky. Anything else? Perfume. Slosh it on. The telephone rang. She answered it. Had he had an accident?

'Hello?' she said.

'Kate, it's Barbara.'

'Oh, Barbara!'

'I've phoned at the wrong time.'

She regained her senses. 'No, you haven't, Barbara. I'm glad you phoned. How are things going?'

'Ralph has had to see the doctor. I can't deal with him any more. He's been taken into hospital.'

'Oh, that's terrible for you! Try not to worry. Would you like me to come and see you?' There was a loud, triumphant ring at her doorbell. She was torn. 'My doorbell, Barbara. I'll phone you back soon.'

She ran to the door, opened it, and there he was, still looking like Gavin, smiling.

'Come in, Sandy.' She saw the black tie, which prompted her. She was in his arms. 'I was so sorry to hear of your father's death.'

'Yes. A blow to all of us, especially my mother. You would have liked him, Kate,' he said, looking down at her.

'Supposing you release me and we have a cup of coffee?'

'Must I?'

Gavin's smile. 'Right. Lead me to the coffee.'

She started first, telling him about Barbara, without hesitation. 'You can see what a time she has had, Sandy. She needs friends. I should go and see her.'

'Where does she live?'

'In Taunton. It's rather nice there.'

'I could get time off. Why don't I drive you there? It would give us time to talk and make plans. And perhaps I could be of help, too.'

This is what Jan's talking about, she thought. A partner.

'That would be good.' They were sitting on the sofa and he had his arm around her. She lifted her coffee cup, feeling cherished, a new experience.

They had a lot of planning to do. First of all, Taunton and Barbara, a nice little jaunt together, and then perhaps a trip to New York to meet his family and another to Glasgow to meet hers, then where would they live? London, with weekends at the cottage? There was so much to talk about. Then they did a tour upstairs to look at the study and the bedroom, where they had to throw themselves down on the bed because they were so exhausted.

They came together without hesitation or awkwardness, and then it was morning and they walked down to the Hare and Hounds after breakfast. They were talking to Judy and Cyril when Jan and Mark arrived, Jan looking flabbergasted at her friend's handsome companion. Everybody liked everybody else. Kate thought Sandy was charming. She could see Jan thought so too.

'We're off to Taunton today to see Barbara Dexter,' she told the others. 'The vicar has been taken into hospital. Sandy has offered to drive me.'

They were waved off by the other four. 'Good luck,' they all said, goodwill wreathing their faces in smiles.